ALSO FROM JERSEY DEVIL PRESS

Shake Away These Constant Days, by Ryan Werner
Love Me, by Danger Slater
Perhaps., by Stephen Schwegler
Screw the Universe, by Stephen Schwegler and Eirik Gumeny
The 2010 Jersey Devil Press Anthology

The Exponential Apocalypse series, by Eirik Gumeny
Exponential Apocalypse
Dead Presidents
High Voltage
Revenge-aroni

The 2015 JERSEY DEVIL PRESS Anthology

Laura Garrison, Online Editor
Samuel Snoek-Brown, Production Editor
Eirik Gumeny, Founding Editor/Publisher

Jersey Devil Press
www.jerseydevilpress.com

THE 2015 JERSEY DEVIL PRESS ANTHOLOGY

The 2015
JERSEY DEVIL PRESS
Anthology

TABLE OF CONTENTS

Bonnie and Clyde, Nicola Belte.. 13

Brace, Jackson Burgess 16

A Robot's Sonnet, Danger Slater 18

Julia and Raul, Ben Nardolilli 28

Paper Heart, Ally Malinenko 37

Brontosaurus, J.D. Hager... 42

The First Last Mermaid Porn Queen, Yvonne Yu............... 54

Bazaar, y.t. sumner   59

Together, We Can Save a Life, Christopher Lettera.............. 63

Godzilla Reading Haiku, Christopher DeWan....................... 71

Girl Eaten by a Tree, Liz Kicak.................................... 74

Unexpecting, Anna Lea Jancewicz 75

Only One Good Reason to Get a Haircut, Sloan Thomas ... 77

Jolly Roger, Michael Sions... 80

Where's the Best BBQ in This Town?, Matthew Myers....... 85

We Left Him with the Dragging Man, Graham Tugwell..... 90

About the Hiding of Buried Treasure, Kimberly Lojewski 103

Vital: A Love Story, Ally Malinenko... 113

FOREWORD

IN THE AUTUMN OF 1989, while the Berlin Wall was getting ready to fall, I was a DJ.

Admittedly, I was not a DJ with a great many listeners. The station's signal barely covered all of campus. But every Thursday night I got to climb the steps to the fifth floor studio in an ancient administrative building and play exactly what I wanted to play for four hours.

For some reason the station had a fairly large collection of indie records coming out of Russia at that time and I played them a lot. I also played a lot of alternative stuff my brother had indoctrinated me in during high school. But mostly — and this will come as no surprise to anyone who knows me — I played Springsteen.

The first song I played on my first show was "Born to Run." From there I tried to be more obscure, going with deep cuts, B-sides, and the like, as well as the occasional bootleg. I liked to play this one version of "The River" from a concert in Newcastle. Springsteen introduced the song by talking about the times he was too scared to go home and face his father, so he'd spend the night talking to his girlfriend on the pay phone and then crash on a friend's porch. He wound up the story by saying, "This song is everybody needs some place to go, on those nights when they can't go home."

About two months into my DJ run, I got a call from one of my listeners. Eight shows in and this was my first call. I just finished playing "Ramrod" and I eagerly picked up the line ready to engage my audience.

The voice on the end of the line simply said, "Sell all your possessions and buy new music." Then he hung up.

Shortly thereafter, I stopped doing my show. Maybe it was that phone call. Maybe it was because I needed more time for other things that were a priority at that age, like wallowing in untreated depression or engaging in dangerous binge-drinking. Either way, I stopped.

I thought back to that phone call a lot twenty years later when I first started sending out short stories. I could handle the rejection I frequently got; what really hurt was that fundamental sense of not being understood — that vague in-between-the-lines sentiment from an editor that said, "I don't understand you," and/or "What the hell is wrong with you?"

In the summer of 2009, I wrote what I thought was the best story ever. It was called "The Werebear Who Wished to Come in from the Rain" and it was about a little girl whose dead father quite literally watches over her. In addition to feeling like I'd crafted a nice piece of fiction, the story also expressed a lot of what I was feeling after experiencing my dad's own death two years earlier. I felt like that story — how it worked on both levels — was everything I wanted to be a writer for.

At the same time, a major science fiction publisher had just issued a call for submissions for an anthology of stories about were-creatures. Coincidence? Of course not. This was the Universe telling me my time had come as a writer!

I made sure my manuscript was formatted exactly as desired. I agonized over my third-person bio. I proofread the text fifty-four times. Finally, I sent it in. And… six hours later I got a rejection back, one of those that had that air of "What the fuck is wrong with you?" about it.

For the next two days, you could've peeled me off a wall.

I was ready to give up on being a writer.

And then… I forced myself to look at the Duotrope listings one more time. And I saw a listing for this new magazine called *Jersey Devil Press*. I don't know why I sent in "Werebear." Maybe it was the Jersey connection… but there was also something about the way they described the stories they wanted that made me want to be part of that magazine, even though it still hadn't published a single issue.

So I sent in my story and within twenty-four hours I got an email back from Eirik Gumeny saying that not only did he want to publish my story, he had to.

And that made all the difference. Not just being accepted, but understood.

A few days after JDP published its first issue, I was at one of the concerts Springsteen played to close down Giants Stadium before it met with the wrecking ball. Unbeknownst to me at the time, Eirik was at the same exact show with his future wife and JDP's co-founder, Monica Rodriguez.

Coincidence? Maybe. But this time I think the Universe really was making a statement.

The idea that there was a magazine out there that got me and my kind — the strange denizens that exist with one foot in the literary world and one foot in a Godzilla slipper — was just so essential. The indie lit world needed an Island of Misfit Toys and JDP would provide it.

That's why after twenty-five great issues, when Eirik stepped down as editor, I stepped in. That tradition of providing a haven for the weird and well-written was still needed. It's why I was so happy when Laura Garrison agreed to keep JDP going after my run as editor ended.

The stories you'll find in these pages are some of the best examples of the citizens that live in the weird little kingdom Eirik, Monica, me, Laura, and our production editor, Sam Snoek-Brown, have cultivated over the past six years. You'll find funny stories, scary stories, straight-up literary stories, and stories that defy categorization. (I'm thinking of you "Brace.")

Hopefully, you'll recognize your own awkward, weird-but-well-written self in here too.

That's what *Jersey Devil Press* is here for.

"Because everybody needs some place to go on those nights when they can't go home."

Mike Sweeney
New Jersey
October 2015

BONNiE AND CLYDE
NiCOLa BeLte

HE SITS UPRIGHT ON HIS HAUNCHES in the middle of the rug, sticks out his paws, and lets his tongue loll from his mouth. No. Too keen. He rolls onto his back, arms and legs in the air, and wriggles on the floor like there's an itch in the middle of his spine. No. Too cute. He sits cross-legged, shoulders slumped, as a fist of sunlight punches through the curtains and raps its knuckles on his head. He feels silly, almost scolded. He just can't get into it today.

He gets on all fours — *that never fails* — and growls, scrambling up as a car door slams shut outside, yanking the curtains together. He can't have them peering in, not after last week. It's bad enough when the postman leaves his packages with his neighbors, but when they "accidentally" open them… He peers out and sees her head bob along above the hedgerow. Nosey bitch. He imagines her in her immaculate kitchen; her lips puckered and her eyebrows near jumping off her face as she pulls his beautiful new tail from the box, like it was gross matted hair from a plughole.

Fence panels, he thinks, *ten foot high ones*. Anticipating all the al-fresco fun that he and Bonnie will then be able to have, he shakes his fluffy head, making the tiny silver bone dangling from his collar bounce.

She's late. He's given up waiting in the middle of the floor; he'll assume position when he hears her key in the door. She hadn't looked impressed when he'd given her a key. He'd covered her eyes, and slipped it into her hands, and she'd looked at it like it was something he'd emptied out of a pooper-scooper, and *then* complained that he'd smudged her nose.

He sighs and slumps down on the lumpy floral sofa. He runs his hands across the greasy armrests, faded and worn from too many nights crashing out when he was too drunk to get to the bedroom — before they'd met, of course.

It's humid, and his suit is beginning to itch. It's dry clean only, and his mother's friend works at the laundry. The last time he went in he'd told her he'd been to a fancy dress party. The time before that he was making balloon poodles in disguise, for the sick kids in the hospital, stuttering and going red as her long nails scratched at the stubborn clumps in the fur.

He drinks a beer. He's hungry, but he wants to wait for her. Their bowls sit next to each other on the floor, filled with pink marshmallow hearts. He thinks of their noses touching as they eat, their bottoms wiggling harmoniously in unison. She must be working late. But surely she'd have called?

She wasn't herself last time. She didn't bother with the whiskers and she'd lost one of her feet. She'd kept going on about the taxi driver, who'd asked her too many questions — who'd stared at her — and then over-charged her, knowing that a raccoon wouldn't argue back.

She'd lain stiff and grumpy in his paws, not yelping or yiffing or mewing or panting, eyes glazed over, like roadkill. She said she was tired, that she had stuff to do, *work stuff*, and that she couldn't be expected to spend all evening sniffing and scratching at each other. She'd said that she rather they just mate quickly, and be done with it, and crouched forward over the bed with her nose in the pillows and her tail in the air.

He calls her and reaches her voicemail, her professional one, and listens to her posh voice that sounds nothing like her. She sounds like a dog trainer, one that reigns with a rolled up newspaper, a stern finger, and a whistle. The girl he knew would bite her.

She was probably out with them. Those men. Those *successful* men. He imagines them all jostling about together in a crowded bar, their knees pressing together under the tables, talking about marketing strategies until the booze kicks in. Human hyenas. Pack animals. Men. His heart races, and he reminds himself that they don't know her, not at all, not like he does.

He'd felt the tips of her tiny ears pricking into his chin as they'd fallen asleep, fingers and limbs intertwined. They hadn't. He'd seen the glittery freckles of glue on her cheeks when her whiskers came off, the way that her tail hung so perfectly between the curves of her buttocks, the shape of her wonderful breasts in her black and white leotard. They hadn't. These things were his and his alone.

He remembers when they met. He hadn't been sure about the party. Chatting online was one thing, but actually meeting those people? He'd sat in his car, tapping the wheel, trying to guess who the furries were amongst the people walking past. *Him? No way. Her? Perhaps. What am I? In or out? Fuck it.* He walked in.

It was meant to be. She, nicknamed Bonnie, named after her grandmother's dead terrier; he, a coyote named Clyde, because it sounded dangerous and wild and edgy, and he was anything but.

"Well, fancy that," she'd said, foxily flicking her tail as they were introduced, and as Clyde looked into Bonnie's black-ringed eyes, and took her paws in his, the huskies and the bears and even that beautiful leopardess blurred into hazy dots on some distant savannah.

She isn't coming. He sits in the back yard, watching his stained white pillowcases blow on the clothesline; the black blurs left by her make-up like the mouths of sad ghosts. Something rustles in the trees. A cat wails. He thinks of her, burrowing in, her lithe striped body moving through the battered dustbin of his soul; sees her running away across the fields with his heart shredded in her teeth. *Bitch.* He pulls off his collar. He's a coyote, not a dog.

He'd howl, but he's forgotten how.

BRACE
Jackson Burgess

SO I DIDN'T START OUT WITH DUCKS. It's not like that. It was when S left for Chicago for her year-long internship. I was so in love, and I convinced myself doing it to anybody else would somehow taint my feelings for her, so I made a rule I could only do it to her. Masturbate, I mean. She never gave me pictures of that sort or anything because we weren't that kind of a couple. You understand. She did, however, have a surfeit of Facebook photos. That's what I came to rely on. She had 735 photos, about 300 of which had been taken in the last couple years. Felt weird jacking off to anything older than that. Like pictures of her when she was a kid. Very creepy. So I had about 300 photos to work with. And they lasted me quite a while — about five months. But eventually they got old, and she was so busy with her internship and such that we hardly talked. And she rarely posted new photos of herself. Hardly ever. So one day I was doing the deed and looking out my window at the park, and there wasn't much going on. It was raining a little, like usual. There was a clown selling balloon animals. Yeah, in the rain. And I was working it and working it, and right when I was about to come, my eyes just happened to fall upon a brace of ducks — that's the correct term: a "brace." There were about six or seven of them. And something about their little feet waddling, their little tails plip-plopping back and forth just made me… happy. Then I came and it was great. Now those ducks were almost always out there — maybe not the same ones, but some always were — and that day felt so good that the next day I waited until I had an ideal vantage point of another brace and then I masturbated. Didn't even need any photos of her or anything. And it was just as good the second time. Their silky, sleek feathers and innocent little eyes… intoxicating. I wasn't doing it *to* the ducks; it was more *at* them. Though I suppose that sounds just as strange. But that's how I survived the year of her absence. Fapping at the ducks. It was when she returned home that I started having problems. I couldn't come with her. It's like without the reassuring presence of my ducks, doing it just didn't feel right. I tried to fix it. I put up pictures of mallard ducks around my desk and on the ceiling, so no matter what position we were in I could see them. It worked, but just barely. It was never the same. Eventually I couldn't stand it anymore, so I spilled my guts. She took it surprisingly well. Looking back, her acceptance was quite a testament to her feelings for me, and she was even willing to try and do it together, *while* looking at the ducks out the window. We moved the bed over and everything. It was… it was the single most sexually gratifying experience of my life. *And she felt the same.* Our duck-fapping became a regular thing. We never told anybody. But one day I walked in and found her. She was alone, doing it herself, looking out at the ducks just like I used to. She had the same glaze-eyed euphoric look. That's how I knew: I was going to be replaced. Now that she'd done it without me, there was just no way I could compare to the ducks' avian charm, their smooth and subtle allure. I knew the ducks' power. She'd realized she didn't need me. And the weirdest part? The only part that worries me? I was okay with that. Being replaced, I mean. So I walked over and sat down and started doing it at the ducks, too. And we did it together. That's how it goes most days, now. We just sit there and masturbate, looking out at the ducks, and we hardly even speak to each other at all. And it feels just as good every time.

A ROBOT'S SONNET
Danger Slater

HE SPITS THE WINE BACK INTO MY FACE.

"Ugh," he gags, thrusting the half-empty glass at me, "what is this garbage?" I inspect it. I dip in a sensor and test it for impurities. I run an hour and a half of diagnostics on it. The results come up clean.

"It's red wine, sir. Just like you asked."

The tiny row of lights that make up my speech-composite box glow chrome-yellow with my reply. I can see it reflecting in the wettest parts of his eyes. The bars at the corners of my mouth illuminate.

So this is what I look like when I smile.

"What are you smirking about, you moron?" he shouts. "I asked for Merlot. This is Cabernet."

"I'm sorry, sir. My data log indicates that you did not specify. You had roast pheasant for dinner. Foodandwine.com lists Cabernet as the most logical pairing."

He growls, showing me his bare teeth — streaked like storm windows by plaque and cigarettes. Make an appointment for a whitening with Dr. Punjab, I note. Also, write a strongly-worded letter to foodandwine.com informing them of their egregious mistake.

"You hunk of junk," he says viciously. "You think you're so goddamn smart. I should sell you for spare parts is what I should do!"

"Please, sir, don't do that. I — I don't know where I'd be without you…" I say. And the words I speak are true, because without Henry, I wouldn't be here today. He built me himself out of a microwave, an electric toothbrush, and a second-generation iPod touch. I recall every vivid detail of that day just as I recall every vivid detail of every day. I come equipped with six terabytes of memory.

Before then there was nothing; just the blackness eternal of my pre-birth — a notion so inconceivable I can feel my circuitry start to overheat should I think about it too hard. So I don't. I don't think about it at all. I keep myself busy, serving my owner, doing my job. I don't think about all there was that existed before me. Or all that might exist after I'm gone.

"Then stop standing there like some kind of slack-jawed cretin and get me my Merlot. NOW!" he screams, throwing the wine glass at the wall. It shatters against the wood-paneled veneer into a million sharp razor-shards that sprinkle the carpet like a sky full of stars.

My Vac-U-Penis® deploys, sucking up the debris, and I wheel myself into the kitchen to get him his drink.

🐜🐜🐜

He doesn't mean to be so [I log onto thesasurus.com, searching the archives for just the right word: crabby, ill-tempered, irritable, querulous]. He's a good man. He's just malfunctioning a bit.

When Sylvia left, he went into a depression. As I understand it, depression is like having your brain stuck in quicksand. You're immobile. Trapped in a moment. And you wiggle and kick and try to fight it, but you just sink deeper. You keep on sinking until you're totally gone.

"Do you know what love is?" he asked me one night. He was on his fifth glass of Noir and the inevitable tears were starting to form.

"I believe I do," I replied. "Love is a feeling of intense desire and affection towards somebody or something whom one is disposed to make a pair."

"Yeah, I know you know the definition of love, but do you *truly* know what it means?"

His head swiveled on his shoulders like it were a bowling ball perched atop a very weak spring. Like he needed a tune-up. Or a new crankshaft.

"Well… no. I suppose I don't," I said.

"I envy you sometimes. You ain't got nothing in this world to hold you down. You're just computer chips and algorithms and for you, everything makes sense." He finished off the glass. "It's difficult to get your heart broken if you don't have one."

"Yes. I don't think I'd be very useful to you, should that be the case."

"I'm glad you're a robot," he said, a single teardrop now streaming down his cheek. "I'm glad to have *something* that won't ever leave me."

That same night, as I charged, I had a dream. It was the first dream I ever dreamt.

I dreamt I was alone, in the middle of a field. The sun was above me, casting off golden rays that reflected off my headplate like it was I who was shining so bright and warm. In the dream, I rolled across the daffodiled landscape, up and down cobbled hills, over gravel and limestone, until I reached a precipice that overlooked the ocean. I stood at the edge of the cliff for a while, just staring out at the sea. The choppy water splashed so soft and rhythmic, should I encode and convert it into musical notes, a thousand violins wouldn't be able to play my song.

I stared out at the sea.

And then I jumped.

***

"Here you go," I say, quickly wheeling myself back into the living room. "Merlot, exactly 62° Fahrenheit."

"Took you long enough, you piece of shit," he barks. "Jesus. I could've crushed the grapes myself by now."

"Yes, but could you have fermented them?" I ask.

"Oh, a wise-ass, eh?" he goes.

"No, sir," I reply, "I do not have an ass."

"Well, if you did I'd be kicking it from here to Timbuktu." He downs the wine in one solid gulp. I opt not to tell him that Timbuktu is exactly 4,441.9 miles away and that it is an impossibly long distance for an ass to be kicked.

***

I wrote his best-selling novel.

You figure it'd be difficult for a robot to create a best-selling work of original fiction, but the truth is no — it's not difficult at all. I only had to log onto Amazon.com's top-sellers list, feed the data into my demodulation cortex, rearrange the adjectives, nouns and verbs, and *voila!* 500 pages burst forth from my inkjet: numbered, Times New Roman, and in double-spaced format.

He found it in the morning; reams of paper in disarray all over the dining room floor.

"What the hell is this?" he said, pointing to the mess. "Don't tell me you're on the fritz again."

"No, sir, I was writing a book," I proudly beamed.

"A book? You? Oh, this has got to be a laugh. So, Chaucer," he mocked me, "what's your little 'book' about?"

"It's a psychological/religious/action/thriller about a guy and a girl in a museum who find some very interesting clues hidden in one of the paintings. I call it *The Picasso Code*."

"You've got to be fucking kidding me."

But then he picked up the first page and read it. His demeanor quickly changed.

"This… This is amazing," he exclaimed, a smile breaking through the fog of his hangover.

"Thank you, sir. I don't know what came over me. I just — I don't know — had to express myself."

"Do you mind if I take this with me today?" he politely asked, the softness in his voice somewhat off-putting, like a bizarre and exotic spice.

"Not at all," I chirped, "I want you to enjoy it, I wrote it for you. To help take your mind off… you know… everything."

He collected up the papers, organizing them carefully, and brought the entire tome to a publishing house in the city. They signed the deal that very evening.

A month later we received an advanced copy in the mail. There it was, my book — *our* book — his name plastered in bold-face across the front cover:

THE PICASSO CODE
A Novel
by HENRY POLANSKI

† † †

"We did it! We did it!" he had said, skipping into the house.

"Good for us," I said. "What exactly did we do?"

"We hit number one. *The Picasso Code* is number one!" He dropped to his knees and gave me a hug, his pink, furry flesh squishing against my alloys. "Did you hear me, you beautiful toolbox? We're a goddamned genius!"

I reached around his body, my frail TV antenna arms hugging him back. An awkward motion. One I'm not accustomed to.

"I'm glad, sir," was all I said. "Your happiness means the world to me."

Then the second novel came out.

Cretaceous Park, our science-fiction/adventure/dinosaur/thriller was received by the critics with relative scorn:

> *Trite... long-winded... overly technical... with language seemingly influenced by children's coloring books and the UNIX Systems operator's manual, Polanski's sophomore release is a blight on the sensibilities of discerning readers everywhere...*

Henry began drinking. Often. And a lot.

"You're worthless," he said one evening, not even bothering to look at me.

"Excuse me?" I asked.

"Excuse you is right!" he snarked. "We barely sold a million copies. Not even a goddamned million!" he shouted, throwing a crumpled up copy of the *New York Times Book Review* at me. When I tried to clean it up, he threw an empty bottle of Sauvignon Blanc at me.

"The public is fickle," I said, trying to console him. "I'm sure there are a multitude of reasons behind their apathy. Just because dino-erotic literature is not what's 'in' right now, it doesn't mean we didn't create a great piece of fiction. And besides, who cares what other people think? Yours is the only opinion that matters to me, sir."

"Yeah? Well here's my opinion, robot: Don't Write Anymore!"

And then he started crying. And from across the room I could see my reflection emblazoned like a neon tattoo in the wettest parts of his eyes.

I was frowning.

Since that day, I haven't written a word.

⚇⚇⚇

He is passed out in the easy chair. Snores a mix of phlegm and gasps slip haphazardly out of his open mouth. The sound resonates across the empty apartment like distant thunder on a collapsing horizon. It is the apex of the night; the hours where only mice and monsters dare to tread and not even the moon has the courage to show its face.

I am in the kitchen — in hibernate mode — when the phone rings.

Brrriiing! Brrriiing! Brrriiing! is what the phone says. My midi-translator [powered by Google] deciphers the phonescreech as a jarring and desperate wail: *Answer me! Answer me! Oh, please, God, won't somebody answer me!* it cries out in agony.

I am not uncouth. I answer the phone.

"Hello?" a grainy female voice in the receiver says.

"Hello," I answer.

"Henry, is that you?" she asks.

"Um…"

I hesitate in my reply. Traditionally, I have not been programmed to speak untruths. Still, as I stutter, something clicks inside me. A desire. A desire to correct an injustice so brazen that it eclipses any peccadillos that might stand in its way. I know who it is on the other end of the line. And I know *exactly* why she's calling.

"… yes," is how I finally respond. "Yes, it's me. Henry."

"You sound different," she says.

"Um, I have a virus."

"Henry, listen," she goes, "I've been doing a lot of soul-searching lately. Reevaluating things — my life and myself. I just… I don't know if breaking up with you was the right thing to do. I miss you, is all. I understand if you're still angry at me. You have every right to be. I was unfair." She exhales somberly. "I'm not looking for peace of mind or your sympathy — but rather — what I'm after is forgiveness. I guess what I'm trying to say is, I'm sorry. I'm sorry, Henry." She sniffles. "And I want you back."

"Oh?"

"And I know any sort of compliment may be a bit late at this point, but I just want you to know that I've been following your writing career very closely. *The Picasso Code* literally brought me to tears. It was brilliant, Henry. Just brilliant! I had no idea you could be so eloquent."

I pause a moment, listening to her breathe, before I ask:

"And what did you think about *Cretaceous Park*?"

"Oh —" she stumbles back on her words like my question were a coffee table she didn't know was there. "It was... um... good."

To this I glower. I seethe and I snarl and I can feel myself boil:

"Now you listen to me, you cold-blooded bitch, and listen up good because I'm only going to say this one fucking time: You need to go away. Get out of my life. Forever. You need to stop poking your goddamn nose where it isn't welcome. I cannot — WILL NOT — let you hurt him again!"

"Him?" she goes.

"Er — um — me. I won't let you hurt *me* again."

"Henry, wait..." she starts, but I don't let her finish. I slam the phone back onto the cradle.

Just a peccadillo, I tell myself. It's for the best.

When I turn, Henry is standing there, cast in shadows. His face half-hidden like a phantom behind the jamb of the door. There is something in his eyes. Something I can't quite define.

Something [thesaurus.com: wicked, baleful, abhorrent, malicious].

"Who was that?" he says quietly, dragging his words.

"No one, sir," I tell him, "just a wrong number."

"A wrong number?" he goes. "You seemed to have an awful lot to talk about with someone who called the wrong number."

"Yes. I was giving them directions. To... uh... Timbuktu."

"You wouldn't be fucking with me, would you, robot?" he says, flicking the wall switch. I am momentarily blinded. When my sight receptors readjust to the new light level, I can see in his hand he holds an axe.

"Because there's a lot you don't understand about being human," he continues, approaching me slowly, using the weapon like it was a cane. *Plink! Plink!* against the linoleum it goes, the sound merely an echo before it reaches my aural decryption unit.

"Emotions are a complex thing," he says, "they're not linear. They're not black and white. They can't be quantified. I guess that's something a machine could never comprehend."

"I wouldn't assume so, sir," I say, nervously rolling backwards until I'm pressed up against the sink.

He holds up the axe, letting the light dance on its point.

"For all the technology the modern world has blessed us with, the beauty of a simple tool can be overlooked quite easily. There's a lot of power in this basic design. A lot of damage could be dealt with just a single blow…"

"Torque," I say.

He slams the axe into the kitchen table, splitting the wood with the ease of a knife through butter.

"Yes, torque," he growls, yanking it back out. He swoops in on me, until only his wretched face fills my lens. His eyebrows twist like crumbling architecture and his pupils have shrunken into two little dots. A black fire burns wild through the whites of his eyes. My facial recognition software can only register his vestige in bits and pieces.

"What did you say to her, huh? What did you say to Sylvia?" he spits, his voice like a minefield, buried bombs on all sides.

I choose what I say next very, very carefully:

"I did what had to be done, sir," I reply. "I can assure you that I only had your well-being in mind. I cannot bear to see you in pain like this any longer. She was a succubus. She left you a shell. And you deserve more. You deserve so much more. Sir, I only did what I did because… because… because I love you."

As I say those words for the first time out loud, ultraviolet waves seem to surge through my circuitry. What is this sensation? I cannot say for certain. There are no words to describe it, no equations to deduce it, no instruments to dissect it. It is something that defies explanation. It's irrational and wonderful and wholly smothering.

From what I've heard, it is called an emotion.

I'm having one right now.

And it is AMAZING!

Oh, the euphoria! The rapture! The sheer essence of *feeling!* In all the days that I've wheeled through life, I've never truly felt so alive!

And just as this epiphany is jolting my mainframe like a million volts of unbridled static-electric joy, Henry lifts up the axe and swings it with all his might.

The blade easily tears through me, plunging straight into my motherboard. My aluminum framework crumples. Safety lights blink and beep. Oil and sparks shoot out of the wound. The rainbow display of my blood pours forth, flashing in Technicolor against the breaking dawn. He puts his weight on the handle and the blade goes deeper.

"How could you do this to me?" he cries, pulling the axe out and swinging it again. And again. And again. And again.

Things are fading. Processors are slowing down. Applications flickering off. He stands back, his chest pumping, watching me fizzle. Smoke. Watching me power down.

And in the moment right before everything disappears, a very strange thought passes through the peripherals of my hard drive. A thought I've spent my entire life trying to ignore. I wondered, where do robots go when they die?

Well, the same place humans go, I suppose.

My lights go out.

And then there is nothing.

☗☗☗

"Ladies and gentlemen, Mr. Henry Polanski," a voice over the loudspeaker announces.

The gathered crowd claps. He gives them a quick wave before taking a seat at the table. The line winds around the bookstore — through the fiction, self-help and biography sections, out into the parking lot. His third novel, *A Robot's Sonnet*, is a critical and commercial success. As it should be. All those newborn, rampant emotions that flowed through me as I lay there dying spewed out my printer in uncontrollable spurts — page upon page of my immortal soul.

> *A profound work of unrepentant empathy... exploring the notion of humanity through a robot's perspective... [Polanski's] latest will surely be the watermark of this — and many — generations to come...*

This is his masterpiece.

My masterpiece.

My final love song to him.

Sylvia stands off to the side, reveling in Henry's abject success. A diamond-encrusted engagement ring sits boisterously on her delicate finger. This book paid for that gaudy piece of jewelry. She talks to his agent as he autographs book sleeves. The agent whispers something into her ear and she laughs, touching him lightly on the arm. A sly look is exchanged between the two — something devious and knowing —

but Henry doesn't notice. He's too busy getting everything he ever wanted.

Best-selling author Henry Polanski. He's finally happy.

And from outside — under the colorless blanket of an overcast sky — I stand, peering in through the storefront window. Watching. Tea kettles and tinfoil and fused together frying pans lay like patchwork over the torn metal scars that cover my body. It's amazing what a little ingenuity and a welding tool can do when somebody puts their mind to it.

I watch the man I so selflessly devoted my entire existence to and I think about all the things happening inside of me. Important things. Complicated things.

Things a man like Henry Polanski will never understand.

I wheel into the bookstore, my gaze holding steady. Slowly, I turn the safety off my machine-gun arms. I log onto thesaurus.com and search through the archives for just the right word:

[vindication, validation, payback, revenge]

If I can't have him, then no one will.

JULIA AND RAUL
BEN NARDOLILLI

JULIA WAS A PENCIL SHARPENER. She was attached to the cinderblock wall of Mrs. Karfunkel's third grade classroom. All of the students had to use her at least once a week. There was no coffee pot or water cooler, so Julia became the place where the students would meet, putting a pencil inside one of her many holes and then exchanging silly stories and knock-knock jokes. Julia was also located in the back of the room, the farthest anyone could get from the teacher without going into the cubby room that was fully hidden from her view.

Julia was made of stainless steel and wore a coat of nickel plating that made her shine across the room. Four screws held her in place. She was completely mechanical. An Amish person could use her, or the students whenever there was a blackout. Julia was a simple, sentient machine. She never got tired of the pencils. She enjoyed the feel of the wood sliding between her teeth, the taste of the paint she slowly chipped away, and the sound the shavings made when they landed in the trash can under her. It was like listening to snow falling.

Sometimes she got very hot because of all the work she did. When there was a test, all the students in the class would get up and sharpen their pencils in her. Some of the students put them in the wrong setting and Julia would have to work extra hard to keep the pencil in place. Occasionally a student would bring a pencil that was new and she had to gnaw on the flat sides of it until it was sharp. Whenever the class bully, Tommy Paterson, had to sharpen his pencil, she made sure that it never got too sharp. One time she had made the mistake of doing her best to make the point of his pencil as sharp as a needle, which Tommy then used to poke the girls in the class. If Tommy kept shoving his writing implement into Julia's mouth and turned her crank in frustration, then she would sometimes bite the end off altogether and send Tommy back to his seat to complete his test in crayon.

The work was enjoyable for her because she got to see the wonderful things the students did with the pencils she sharpened. Their assignments and creative endeavors were often hung on a bulletin board that was made of soft cork, right next to Julia. Sometimes she was able to take pleasure in the simple curves that the students used to imitate the black letters that wrapped around the top of the classroom. Or she could enjoy the high scoring multiplication tests that Mrs. Karfunkel pinned up with gold stars attached to them. The best thing to look at were the drawings the students made of what they were learning, of Pilgrims and Indians, Egyptians and pyramids, or knights and castles. None of it was possible without her and she was happy to be of service.

One day a freckled girl with auburn colored pigtails came over to Julia with a pencil that needed to be sharpened. It was a new one that had been given to her by her grandmother as part of a plethora of school supplies the elderly woman gave her for her birthday. The pigtailed girl was happy to receive them, but wished that the present had included a toy or something edible.

The pencil was different from the others that Julia was used to. Its body was green instead of the bright yellow that matched the color of the school buses that Julia could sometimes see going by in the window. It was flat on the top and had no eraser. Whoever used it could make no mistakes. Julia waited as the pigtailed girl tried to figure out which of the settings was right for the pencil to go through and she felt the cold glossy skin of the pencil between the spinning blades of her throat. The girl's small fingers turned Julia's crank and the pencil ground inside her.

Soon the friction wore away the top and brought the wood out, with a charcoal colored top that was pointed and ready to make letters, lines, and numbers. Julia was ready to let the pencil out but the girl reached for a nearby box of tissues to blow her nose, keeping the sharpened stick inside her. Julia sighed and looked at the pencil inside her. She could only see its green body. She could feel the sharpened parts, but they were hidden from her view.

"Hello."

Julia looked around.

"Hello," the same voice said again. It rumbled and echoed inside her, and she knew then that it was the pencil.

"Hi."

"I'm Raul."

"Oh. I'm Julia."

"Nice to meet you. Thanks for sharpening me."

"No problem."

"All the other pencils were laughing at me. The pens too, but they're always such jerks."

"I never meet many of them."

"I guess you don't. I've heard that being inside one of you guys is like hell, but you were actually very gentle and soft, I barely felt anything."

"You're welcome."

"I bet lots of pencils say that to you."

"No, actually none of them ever talk to me. They just get sharpened and leave."

"They don't ever tell you how smooth the grooves inside you are, or how quiet your gears turn?"

"Nope."

"Well, I guess I am pleased to be the first."

"Good."

"It's getting hot in here. You're not moving, right? I mean, that's not friction."

"Oh, I don't know."

"You're not blushing… are you?"

The girl was done blowing her nose and she removed Raul from the slot inside. Julia looked at him. His owner was holding him up upright, with the sharpened point up in the air. She had never seen a lovelier pencil. He was thin, tall, and his sharp graphite coif was the cleanest and shiniest she had ever seen. Raul took a bow towards Julia in the girl's hands. Julia had never felt so hot after sharpening a pencil before.

The next week, Raul was back. Julia received him gleefully, but spun her gears a little slower so that her metal teeth could run over Raul's body just a little longer. Julia talked to him while he was being sharpened.

"That feels good, Julia."

"What does?"

"When you go slower. I mean I like fast too, and normal, I like all of your settings, but slow is really good. I think it is my favorite."

"You're welcome."

"Julia, is there anything I could do for you?"

"I don't think so."

"Nothing to make it easier on you?"

"No, no, I enjoy the work."

"What if I spin against your little blades?"

"What?"

"Let me try it."

With that, Raul spun himself against the turn of the gears and wheels with riffled edges that were inside Julia. She loved it. It was the most wonderful feeling she had ever had. No pencil, regular or colored, had ever made the insides of her tingle. The pigtailed girl had to stop because it was getting too tiresome to keep spinning the pencil and the sharpener simultaneously. Her wrist and fingers were getting sore. She decided to pull Raul out. She grabbed his body with a pinch and with her other hand tried to get some leverage out of Julia. Once her hand touched the nickel plating, she gave a slight yelp.

Mrs. Karfunkel turned around from the chalkboard at the head of the classroom. "What is it, Jane?"

"Oh, nothing. The pencil sharpener is really hot." She waved her hand to cool it off.

"Well, I think you've been using it for too long, why don't you take a seat?"

Jane obeyed and walked to her desk. Raul was in her hand during the trip and he waved his body at Julia to let her know he was thinking of her and regretted having their meeting disturbed.

While she cooled down, she looked out across the classroom at Jane. She saw her holding Raul and she was angry with her. Her hands often rubbed her nose and then touched Raul's otherwise immaculate green body. She held him as if he was a weapon, a blunt object that she would use to hammer out her letters. She put so much pressure on him that Julia was afraid his top would snap right off or, worse, that he would break in half.

But Raul took his sufferings and his scratching as best as he good. He leaned and squeezed himself within Jane's hand so that he would not make squeaking or screeching sounds, which he was sure Julia found irritating. She appreciated the effort, but still she was sad. She wanted Raul to be near her, inside her if possible. There was something about him which made being apart almost unbearable. It was a form of torture she had never experienced in all her years in Mrs.

Karfunkel's class. She suffered, but never enough that it would completely overwhelm her. She still had the pleasure of thinking of him, and this was enough to let her carry on to the next moment. Her heart felt like it was breaking when in reality it was only her gears growing dusty, longing for him.

The pencil continued through the rest of the day making drawings for Jane and when the teacher was not looking, doodles. Raul wrote a love note for her to give to Tommy Paterson, but was so disgusted with the thought of anyone having a crush on such a bully, that Raul snapped his writing top off deliberately. The sound shocked Jane and she dropped Raul. He rolled until he landed in front of Tommy's worn shoes. Tommy picked him up and smiled at Jane, who blushed as she took the pencil from him. The teacher told both of her students to face forward and they continued to learn about long division.

Raul was put inside the desk with the other pencils. They disliked the attention he had been getting and that he had hurt himself rather than be an instrument for his owner. This was something pencils were not supposed to do. If they had known about him and Julia, they would have been even angrier with him and tempted to cover him in glue if he continued to be troublesome.

Raul hated being in the desk. It was dark and he had no idea what was going on in the rest of the world. It smelled like old rubber and banana peels. Jane had taken another pencil and Raul could hear him writing whatever she wanted. The point ran above him like the dull blade on a pair of ice skates. He could not see it, but he knew it was there being drawn over a piece of paper, line after line.

There was nothing Raul could do except sit and wait. But his pigtailed owner would never pick him because he had made himself blunt and could make no useful marks for her. The bell rang and the knees and thighs of the pigtailed girl that had been so close to him now were gone altogether. The class was going to lunch and then recess. A pair of heels left along with everyone else. There were no human eyes left in the room. Raul decided he had to act.

"Hey, Percy!"

"What?"

"Do you think you could do me a favor?"

"No."

"I want you to come down here so I can try and get up there."

"Why?"

"I just want to."

"No. I'm not going anywhere. You're a bad pencil."

Raul rolled through the plastic surface of the desk and found his friend, Yolanda, who was an eraser. She was shaped like a parallelogram and was bright pink and lived in the desk. They were friends. Yolanda helped to clean up all the marks that Raul left behind. They helped to make each other useful.

"Yolanda?"

"Yes, Raul?"

"I need your help, I want to get on top of the desk."

"Why?"

"Because I... I want to be held by Jane."

"I thought I was the only one for you," she jokingly said.

"Well, she is just so... comfortable and powerful."

"You pencils are all alike, you fall for anything big. You guys have to stand up for yourselves."

"I know, I know, but the revolution will have to wait. I need to get up there and knock Percy out."

"Percy is up there?"

"Yes."

"Percy, Mr. I-Have-My-Own-Eraser-And-Don't-Need-You-Or-Anyone-Else?"

"Yes. I believe that is his maiden name."

"Okay, I'll help you."

The other pencils had gone into the neon orange box that was wide and narrow enough for them to fit in. It was their own private club. Percy was left all alone on top of the desk. Yolanda moved a ruler with Raul's help and they drew it out like a plank to the top of the chair that Jane had slid right next to the desk. Soon the ruler was touching the inside of the desk as well as the top of the chair and Yolanda gave a big push to Raul, who rolled up the ruler and then held himself from going over and falling to the floor.

"All right, Yolanda, press hard and downward on your end of the ruler so that it will fall and send me flying to the desk." He had gotten the idea from pictures of catapults and trebuchets in Jane's history textbook.

Yolanda followed the instructions and the ruler fell, propelling Raul forward. He landed on the desk and rolled over the faux wood finish. There was nothing to stop him until he got to Percy, who was taking a nap. When he woke up, it was too late. Raul's green skin bumped up against his yellow one and Percy absorbed all of Raul's movement. He began to roll as Raul came to a stop, heading all the way to the edge of the desk and falling off.

When recess was over, Jane had gotten to the head of the line through some pushing and shoving that the teacher did not see, her eyes distracted by the gardener's firm arms planting marigolds outside. Jane ran ahead of the rest of the students and saw that her desk was a mess. She had no memory of leaving Raul the green pencil out, but she figured it was a trick and that it was best to put everything back the way it was before anyone saw the ruler and Percy on the floor.

But Raul was still blunt and would have to be sharpened again. Jane picked him up and went over to Julia who was looking brighter than she had ever seen her. Jane figured that the janitor must have come and given her a nice shine. She knew that he sometimes came when no one else was around to make things nice. He must have knocked over her things when he was leaving. Jane slid Raul into the proper hole and began to grind the wheels inside Julia in order to sharpen him.

Julia was ecstatic, she wanted this moment between them to last forever. Raul wanted it too. They held on and spun in opposite directions from one another once more. Julia was starting to heat up. The handle on her crank was plastic, so Jane could not feel it. But the pencil shavings that were still inside her from Raul and those who had come before him, yet had left nothing else behind, started to smoke a bit. Luckily they fell out before they could start a fire. The air was dense between the two lovers and Raul continued to go deeper and deeper into Julia, even as his shiny rear end began to come closer to his tip.

Jane realized that the sharpener was eating up her pencil and decided she had to get it out or else it would soon disappear inside her. She decided not to touch Julia because she did not want to burn her hand again. Julia felt her gear stop and knew that Jane was done.

"My love…"

"Don't worry, I will continue to spin into you, until I vanish. I cannot go back to her."

"Raul…"

He was about to begin spinning on his own, but Jane grabbed him and started to pull him out. He shook and did his best to stop, banging from side to side. Jane pulled harder. When Raul had jammed himself into Julia by leaning to one side, Jane just changed direction and continued to drag him. She thought it was like playing a game of pull the tail off the donkey.

"Come out! Come out!"

"Jane, what's the matter?"

"The stupid sharpener. My pencil is stuck."

"Please do it quietly or don't do it at all, Jane."

She calmed down and let go of the pencil that was now hanging out of Julia at an angle.

"I think she's gone, Julia, I think we're alone now."

But Jane gave the green end of the pencil one final tug. Raul came flying out of the sharpener and out of Jane's hands. The pencil looked back at Julia with the fluorescent light overhead giving a nice gleam to his sharpened head. Jane's auburn pigtails fluttered and her pale hand reached out to try and grab him but he was too fast for her. Raul wanted to take another pencil hostage and draw a smile on his face. He was happy.

Raul left a mark on the whitewashed cinderblocks right across from the pencil sharpener. He actually left two because the force of impact had split him in half. They were very faint marks, but could be seen by anyone who paused for a moment in front of that particular space and stared. Jane was angry. No part of Raul was usable. The top half had a fissure down the middle and the bottom part was too jagged to be held in place long enough to be sharpened.

She tossed him in the garbage can beneath the sharpener. Raul regained some consciousness and realized that his body was broken. His sharpened top was sitting upward as he surveyed what was around him. This was the end for him. There was no one to help him, no one to save him. The remains of fellow pencils were all around him; they had been sharpened down so far that they were no longer useful. But mostly he was surrounded by the shavings that Julia let out from under her.

"My love, my love…"

Julia looked down and saw Raul struggling to see her. She tried to bend quietly so that no one would notice, but it was hard. She moved a little more than she was used to and was surprised. The screws had become loose because of all the extra heat she had given off and the tugging that Jane and all the students before her had put them through. She pressed further and, though she was held back, the restraints were weaker than ever before. Raul was in the trash can still, and neither had a good view of the other. Julia looked over and saw the class was busy having story time. She continued to bend herself.

One screw was gone, it fell out and it landed in the trash can with Raul. Julia did not see where it landed but hoped it did not hit him on the head. Soon she shook another screw loose, and then one more. There was a single screw left and it was the most firm in its place. Julia now hung under it, dangling in the air over the trash can and trying to call out to Raul to let him know she was coming.

Julia kept swinging and even though any of the students or the teacher would have seen her tracing wide arcs in the air, nobody noticed because they were engrossed in the story about a boy who was trying to find a dragon that had belonged to his father. Julia could feel the edge of the screw going thin and friction finally eating its way through it. Her weight was starting to sink her closer and closer to the trash can. Julia took a deep breath and took in all the air she could. She blew out hard and went backward, spinning the whole way around the screw in a full circle. When she came down to where she had started, she had cut herself off from the small metal holder and gravity could now do its work to bring the two lovers together.

Julia sailed through the air and when she landed in the trash can, the sound went ignored by the class. She heard only laughter from them and while they were busy, she looked down, Raul was nowhere to be found. She called out for him but there was no response. Then he started laughing and the vibrations from it filled her insides. She saw a green tip sticking out from the hole in her front. There was never a more perfect fall.

PAPER HEART
ALLY MALINENKO

WHEN SHE WAS BORN the doctors suggested she not be named. She wouldn't last the night. No one had seen anything like it. *Ectopia Cordis* was an extremely rare disorder, a child born with their heart on the outside of their chest. But even then it is always at least flesh and blood. It is always a pulpy red organ.

What Mr. and Mrs. Kagit saw on their daughter was not. They called in the specialists who did not speak Turkish.

"But I don't understand," Mr. Kagit said, careful to speak slowly so as to not trip over his accent.

"Neither do we," the doctor said. He still wore his scrubs and Mr. Kagit, who fiddled with the hat in his hand, couldn't stop his eyes from darting down to the blood and then back to the doctor's face. Blood. So much blood.

"Is she all right?"

"Your wife?"

He nodded. One at a time. His feet were sweating in the plastic booties.

"We must warn you. Mr. Kagit, the child will probably not survive the night," the doctor said on his way back through the swinging doors.

Later, by his wife's side, he held the child. Her dark eyes, stared up at him, a wintery midnight cold. She didn't seem to blink. Nor did she fuss. On her chest, the child's small heart expanded and contracted, crinkling, made of paper, like an origami box. It was white and seemed to have the exact consistency of tissue paper. He lifted a finger, wondering.

"Don't touch it," his wife said, stirring in her sleep. "They said she will not survive."

"Shhhhh," he soothed his wife. Her eyes closed and he brought his daughter closer to his body as if he could pass to her something real, something red and liquid. Something organic. His daughter. With her paper heart.

The reporters came when she survived the night. Then the vigils started. There were candles and weeping women. Baby Kagit was declared a miracle.

More specialists arrived from Istanbul. They took the child and laid her on cold metal and with more cold metal they poked and touched at her beating paper heart. She did not stir. She did not cry. In fact, she had yet to make a sound.

"We're sorry," the specialists said, passing the child back to her mother. "She will not survive. One cannot live with a paper heart. There is nothing we can do." The specialists packed up and left town that night.

They loved her hard and fast, knowing she would not survive. But she did. After the first week they started to wonder, what if? They asked the doctors again but their answer never changed. She cannot live with a paper heart. When a week turned into a month, they named her, Narin Kagit.

When she was two months, they began to play music for her, watching her little paper heart flutter with excitement.

When she turned a year old, the whole town had a celebration; long lines of people filled the dusty streets, their hands full of warm food covered with cloth. The doctors let the Kagit family go home. Why not? Her one year was like a lifetime to most. Each morning, when Mr. Kagit lifted darling Narin out of her crib, her mouth still quiet, her throat fluttering but soundless, her eyes bright and laughing, it was a gift. They doted on her, they loved her, they kissed the dark hair that grew on her head. They kissed her downy eyelids, her round cheeks. They kissed her slender toes, her long arms. At night they wondered, inside never aloud, what she would have looked like if she were able to grow. Her warm mocha skin, her dark hair, her black black eyes. She would have her mother's beauty and her father's strength. She would have the best of both of them.

They performed a ziyarat and took her to the türbe, lifted her in the air, and pressed her face against the chalky stone. Even then she did not make a sound. They prayed hard and fast for a cure.

When she turned two, they had another celebration. She was a blessed thing. A child of great importance. She was a message from Allah, from the Great Spirit. The town gathered to watch her walk and run, Narin's dark hair flowing behind her, her paper heart fluttering. She must be a message, they said, a message from the heavens. We should all live so free, they said. Praise, Allah. She's a prophet. Will she ever speak?

When she turned five, they decided, with a shrug of their shoulders, that she should go to school. What choice was there? So they packed her a small lunch and brought her to the schoolhouse.

"Don't let anyone touch your heart, okay taçyaprağı?" her father said. He drew with a finger a little circle around her chest and she nodded. "And you stay far from the water, okay?" The water would melt her paper heart, turning it to mush and stopping whatever force flowed through her veins.

As so she did. And the years came and went and came and went and Narin grew up, tall with a strong spine and long fingers and dark hair and black bottomless eyes. And eventually they all stopped thinking of her as their little miracle and the people of the town went back to work, back to their lives and when she passed them on the street they nodded as custom instead of gesticulating and kissing her palm which was by all means, just fine with Narin.

But still she didn't speak. She carried a slate at her hip and an endless supply of chalk was always dusting everything she touched and leaving little pocks of powder along her cheek or the back of her hands. She seemed unable to speak. Or unwilling. Her parents assumed it was part of her condition. A paper heart and no voice. But still, Narin was happy and light and good.

The day he arrived was just like any other. He hadn't planned on coming to this town, he told her later, but he hadn't planned anything, he said often and with a sigh.

His name was Damla and he did not know his parents. He was thin, wiry, as if his body had been stretched too far over his delicate years. He had no memory of his parents. Only of the orphanage, the hot kitchen, later the workhouse. He left when he was eleven and had been walking ever since. He worked when he could and he walked. He couldn't remember how old he was.

He could not read so when Narin wrote on her tablet he shook his head. Instead he just stared into her eyes and she into his and they understood one another as millions of lovers have for centuries. Damla, like Narin, was born different. But he was never thought to be a message from Allah. Born without tear ducts his eyes leaked all the time. Even when he smiled, even when he slept, glistening tears, dripped down his face, staining his skin, like a river corroding rock. In the workhouses of other towns, they called him the devil. "Serpent tears," they hissed, spitting at the floor near his feet.

"I cannot stop," he told her, dabbing a stained cloth at his eyes. "I am always crying."

The first time they made love, she unbuttoned her shirt. Her breasts hung delicate and light, her nipples turned upward. Between them her paper heart fluttered. She climbed on top, and when he entered her, he touched her briefly, one slender finger just brushing her paper heart. His tears formed a halo around his head, staining the blanket.

They were not to be together, so naturally they always were. He wore no shoes so that he could steal into her home and climb into her bed. When he left she touched the warm dark spots on the pillow, left by his tears. He told her she was beautiful, kissed her slender arms, the nape of her warm neck, the hollow of her throat. He traveled down her body carefully, always so careful to not let a single tear fall on her paper heart.

"Leave with me," he told her under a sky like a soap bubble. Damla propped himself up on one elbow, his long hair brushing his shoulder. The tears fell, one two, landing on the side of Narin's cheek as she gazed up at him. "Leave with me."

She shook her head and smiled, always smiled. Her sweet Damla, with his big plans.

"We can run away together. We can leave here," he begged.

She pulled him to her, her mouth closing over his to keep all those words inside. He kissed her back, pulled her on top of him, her paper heart fluttering.

But Damla had been right. They should have left. One miracle can bless a town, give it new life, and inflate it like a paper lantern to create a light against the darkness. But two miracles rub up hard against luck. Two miracles are suspicious, greedy. And a third miracle, secret love, is the most suspicious of all.

Towns talk. After the rains, they pull from the mud all the things that people bury. They pull up gravestones and fear. They pull up broken toys and hope. Sometimes they pull up lies and suspicion.

The fire started in the workman's camp where Damla should have been sleeping. Should have, but wasn't because Damla was in the poppy field, naked and entwined. The smoke rose like a living thing, tamping out the sky. The flames, new to this world and hungry, licked and tasted everything they could find. They even licked the workers whose screams reached the ears of the two lovers in the poppies. Narin and Damla dressed hastily, racing hand in hand towards all that death and destruction. By then people had gathered, passing bucket after bucket after bucket to try and snuff out the flames. Narin saw her father, sweat on his face, his hands shaking as he passed bucket after bucket after bucket and he saw her. He saw her quickly unclasp hands with the boy. He saw her shirt mis-buttoned so that the collar was split wide and through it one could see the slightest crinkle of fluttering paper.

And the rest of the town saw it too. One miracle is a good thing. Two is spoiling it.

The people saw Narin, her clothing askew, her hair wild, tangled with bits of grass. They saw her now as a woman; as a dangerous woman. No longer was she theirs alone, their gift from Allah. And next to her, they saw Damla, the stranger, whose hands did not clutch bucket after bucket after bucket of sloshing water. Instead they wiped at his face, at his serpent tears which continued to fall, now mocking their pain. And they decided that he had taken too much. First, their sweet Narin and then their peace. He could not stay.

When the smoke cleared, the bodies lay scorched and still. Raw skin bubbled and popped. The death smell drifted everywhere. Eventually, it was all that they could smell.

When they threatened him, she did not speak. When they banished him, she did not speak. Damla did as he always did, took to the road, one foot and then another and then another.

"I told you not to let anyone touch your heart, taçyaprağı," her father whispered as they watched the boy with the serpent tears leave. The soap bubble sky popped. Her father did not stay to hear her first words, created by sorrow and birthed in pain, the harsh guttural words of a torn paper heart. When she cried, she let the tears fall until it turned first pulpy and then red and then, strangely organic.

BRONTOSAURUS
J.D. Hager

JACOB SPOKE HIS FIRST WORDS at the breakfast table, the day after he turned six. On his breakfast plate stood an intricate double-frosted dinosaur made of Pop-Tarts and banana, three dimensional and freestanding, a marvel of breakfast engineering.

"Brontosaurus," Jacob said to his breakfast sculpture. A moment later he followed with "Tyrannosaurus" and then leaned in to bite the head off his poptartosaurus. Jacob sat back up and looked at his father snarling, his teeth covered in raspberry-flavored Pop-Tart filling.

Higgins felt surprised, relieved, and slightly disgusted. He wanted to ask Jacob where he learned those multisyllabic words, but suddenly Higgins was the one who couldn't speak. By the time his son turned six, Higgins had given up hope of hearing Jacob say anything and barely spoke himself anymore. He spent hours in silence wondering how his son would make it through life without the use of words.

Jacob always had a fascination with animals, but especially dinosaurs. Whenever he saw one in a picture book he would reach out and touch it with his finger. After his first words that morning Jacob began speaking the names of many other types of dinosaur. His entire spoken vocabulary consisted of nothing but dinosaur names, and eventually his father began to understand what each meant. Tyrannosaurus meant he was hungry. Iguanodon meant he was tired. Triceratops meant he wanted to go play outside. But Brontosaurus seemed to mean nothing and everything at the same time. He said it whenever he was excited or throwing a tantrum. He would walk in circles repeating it over and over like a monk in a trance. Sometimes he would just look at Higgins with sleepy eyes and say *Brontosaurus*, and Higgins knew it was Jacob's way of saying *I love you*.

Things hadn't always been so quiet in the house. Higgins and his wife Lulu used to speak to Jacob after he was born, baby talk and other types of first-time parental pandering. Higgins' personal favorite was *who's got a belly button* as he poked Jacob like a little marshmallow. They doted and squealed the way most first time parents do, but Jacob barely noticed. They thought he might be deaf or mute, but doctors assured them his hearing was excellent. Perhaps there were other issues doctors told them. Perhaps he was on the spectrum. They soon noticed other complications. Jacob never laughed or smiled, and as soon as he learned to walk he started spending hours pacing in circles. Still Higgins and Lulu were hopeful, and she would sing and read to Jacob and talk to him daily. But one day something broke inside of her and her hope abandoned her.

Higgins often thought back to the night Jacob was born. Lulu's water broke minutes after they said their *I dos*, and Jacob entered the world in the lobby of city hall. Lulu's labor lasted only twenty-three minutes, and Jacob had practically leapt from her womb. But even more surprising, Jacob hadn't cried at all. Higgins had wrapped his son in a *Welcome to Ketchum* sweatshirt the presiding judge had provided and stared lovingly into his son's eyes. Jacob just looked back at him, no tears, no crying, nothing but Jacob's cloudy blues gazing back at him like a mute little sage. For Higgins this moment was as vivid as if it was still happening.

Later, as the paramedics rolled Lulu and Jacob toward the ambulance, she grabbed Higgins' hand with desperate strength and told him she would never divorce him. For a moment he mistook this for an impromptu vow, but then she continued. She said she hated long goodbyes, and if there was ever a problem she would just leave.

On a Tuesday about seventeen months ago, Higgins noticed his wife's luggage and jewelry box were gone. He found her wedding ring sitting on the bedside table with no note. It took a while for the truth of the situation to sink in, and even now it was still sinking. He woke up every morning and looked out his bedroom window with a sad hope, imagining her pulling back into the driveway with a perfect explanation of the entire absence, so their tragic autistic life could continue as if nothing had ever happened.

After she left, the house fell into complete silence. The phone never rang. No vacuum salesmen or Jehovah's witnesses knocked on the door. All communications between Higgins and his son were done with hand gestures and facial expressions. At times they even approached telepathic communication, a powerful father-son connection beyond mere eye contact and sign language. They concluded each interaction with a silent fist bump, the brief physical contact bridging the unspoken distance between them.

Higgins got a dog, hoping the barking and other dog sounds might break the monastic silence, but the dog was just as quiet as his son. Jacob started calling the dog Brontosaurus, Bronto for short. Bronto was a mutt from the shelter, a fuzzy little teddy bear with a mullet. Jacob bonded with the dog immediately, and the two of them would sit together and silently stare at things, especially Higgins. Higgins feared the dog might be autistic also.

But all those years of nonverbal desolation changed the moment Jacob spoke that first word. Brontosaurus.

Jacob found a tabloid in the back of the hallway closet buried under other forgotten and embarrassing items. He repeated *Brontosaurus, Brontosaurus, Brontosaurus* as he waved the old newsprint in Higgins' face. Jacob had discovered something exciting inside, wedged between stories of a Chupacabra epidemic and a dog elected mayor of a town in Minnesota.

"Brontosaurus," he repeated, touching a tiny black and white picture of a dinosaur with his finger. It was an ad for *Real Live Dinosaur Eggs*. There was a photo of an oblong, polka-dot egg, and standing behind was a long-necked dinosaur in a graceful, symmetrical pose. The ad went on about *exciting new advances in genetics* and *authentic Apatosaurus ajax DNA*. It claimed *now available to public for a limited time*. There was a microscopic disclaimer at the bottom of the ad. **Eggs sterile — now guaranteed not to hatch*, as if there had been some accidental hatchings in the past.

"Brontosaurus," Jacob repeated, looking at Higgins with hopeful eyes, sending a telepathic message of desire. Hope and desire were something new for Jacob. It felt promising.

"Yep," Higgins said, "Brontosaurus."

Higgins wondered where his son learned those dinosaur names in the first place. He must have heard them watching the Discovery Channel, or remembered them from one of the dinosaur books Lulu had read to him hundreds of times. Jacob never had any formal schooling, and couldn't read or write as far as Higgins knew. Lulu had plans to home school Jacob, educate him while protecting him from the indecency of public schools and special ed. But after she left, Jacob's home-schooling plans took a nosedive that mirrored Higgins' own descent. Higgins' job in scripts and hypertexts allowed him to work from home, and the daily distraction of work saved him from a total meltdown. He found refuge in the code. But Higgins had been so busy working and feeling sorry for himself that he forgot to register Jacob for kindergarten. After the deadline had passed, Higgins considered homeschooling Jacob himself, but suspected he was the worst teacher in Idaho. Together he and Jacob were less than hopeless, but apart they'd be even lower.

After a moment that felt more silent than normal, Jacob said, "Live dinosaur hatch." It dawned on Higgins that his son must be reading the words. Not only that, he had spoken a verb and an adjective. Perhaps he and Jacob were not as hopeless as he thought.

The dinosaur eggs arrived eleven days later. They looked smaller than Higgins expected and weren't even polka-dotted. They were leathery and squishy and reminded him of sea turtle eggs he'd seen in Mexico. He felt swindled, and stupid for buying three just to get free shipping. He wondered if he should even show them to Jacob, if Jacob would be as disappointed as he was. Just as Higgins decided to place them back into their bubble-wrapped box and never mention them again, Jacob walked in. He saw Higgins holding an egg and trying to stuff it back in the box. Jacob raised one eyebrow and gave his father a puzzled look, mimicking perfectly the curious look his father flashed when Higgins wasn't sure what his son was up to.

Higgins just looked at him and shrugged his shoulders. Finally he said, "Brontosaurus."

"Brontosaurus?" Jacob asked.

Higgins nodded his head.

"Live egg hatch?" Jacob asked.

Higgins shrugged his shoulders.

"Brontosaurus!"

Higgins didn't want to get Jacob's hopes up, but the look of joy in his son's eyes was more amazing than Higgins ever imagined. Jacob even displayed a slight upturn at the corners of his mouth that Higgins recognized as a smile despite its repressed and fleeting nature. Higgins decided the eggs were worth every penny whether they hatched or not.

Jacob found purpose in those eggs. He took them to his sandbox and buried them with exaggerated care. He constructed a small protective structure out of twigs and acorns, and guarded and doted over them like he himself had laid them. Higgins knew the eggs would never hatch, and wondered how long Jacob's focused protection would continue. Would he give up hope? Would his next emotional lesson be disappointment?

About a year after Lulu left, envelopes of cash started appearing in the mailbox. Normally it was $200, twenties and tens double wrapped in plastic. Higgins pretended to wonder who was sending the money. *What angel of mercy has blessed us?* he asked the universe, looking around like the angel might be lurking nearby. The envelopes never had a return address, and the postmarks came from different locations every time. Once it was Lone Pine, CA, and next it was Salem, OR. Usually they came from Nevada, which convinced Higgins his wife was back in Vegas and dancing again.

The latest double-wrapped stack of cash arrived sealed in a blank envelope with no visible marks on the outside. No address, no stamp, no bar codes or tracking numbers. His wife was close, probably watching in the bushes with binoculars and a cigarette. This just fueled Higgins' delusions of her eventual return.

Soon after the first envelopes arrived they also had a visitor from the *Idaho Coalition of Home Educators*, a social worker whose glasses and haircut made her resemble a female Harry Potter. She'd come to investigate a complaint of inadequate homeschooling curriculum. Higgins asked who filed the complaint, but his question was ignored. She instead asked to speak to Jacob. Higgins took her to the backyard where Jacob hunkered down in the sandbox, protecting his eggs.

"Hello, Jacob," she said. "My name is Marcy. I'm here to ask some questions about what you're learning at homeschool."

Higgins looked at Jacob guarding his eggs, wondering what Marcy must think. Jacob's T-shirt was filthy, and he wasn't wearing any pants, only saggy, old underwear. He started every day wearing pants and then somewhere along the line, no pants. Higgins also noticed how long it had been since Jacob's last haircut, and his son's tangled blond mop made him look feral and untamed. Jacob squatted over his nest in his underwear and looked at Higgins and the social worker like they were lunch. He jumped up and let out a high-pitched noise that sounded like Godzilla on helium.

"We bought some dinosaur eggs," Higgins said. "He's very protective."

"Do you like dinosaurs?" she asked. Marcy took a couple steps toward Jacob, and he coiled back like a serpent preparing to strike. "What's your favorite dinosaur?"

"Brontosaurus!" he said, followed this time by a series of noises that sounded like the mating call of some large, possibly extinct species of bird.

What were the chances she would ask Jacob the only question he could actually answer? Higgins decided to say something before things turned even more awkward.

"You know he's autistic, right?"

Marcy turned and looked at Higgins for a moment like she didn't understand. She scribbled something in her notebook and then turned back toward Jacob.

"What else have you been studying besides dinosaurs, Jacob?"

"Brontosaurus."

"Are you learning any math, Jacob? Numbers?"

"Brontosaurus, brontosaurus, brontosaurus!"

"That's how he counts to three," Higgins said. This wasn't true, but it sounded good.

Marcy turned and gave Higgins another look, and scribbled into her notebook again, only this time she wrote more. "How old are you, Jacob?"

"Brontosaurus, brontosaurus, brontosaurus, brontosaurus, brontosaurus, brontosaurus." Even though he could barely speak, Jacob always seemed to understand.

Marcy looked back to Higgins like she needed a translation. "I was told he was seven. Is he actually six?" Higgins decided he should just keep his mouth shut and nodded like a bobblehead.

Higgins learned the state of Idaho didn't require either home or public schooling until the age of seven, which gave him six months before it officially became a case of child negligence. Marcy gave him the brochure for an academy in Boise for autistic children. She left information about the rights of students with learning disabilities and an outline of curriculum expected for home-schooled children. As Jacob walked in circles around his sandbox squawking like a bird, Marcy promised to return in six months to check on his progress.

Higgins knew something was amiss. He first heard Bronto barking, induced into a surprisingly loud barking fit by some sort of evil presence in the backyard. Then Higgins heard laughing. The joyous laughter of a child, in particular his child, which was more shocking than the barks of little Bronto.

Higgins hurried into the backyard to investigate. He noticed the eggs in the sand box, the leathery shell left behind like wads of crumpled tissue. He followed the barking and laughing to the back corner of the yard, where Bronto had something pinned against the fence while Jacob laughed and clapped his hands hysterically.

"Jacob?"

His son and the dog both turned and looked at Higgins, cocking their heads to the side in unison. He wanted to take a picture of that moment, put it on a postcard and send it to his wife, wherever she was.

"Brontosaurus!" Jacob yelled, between his squeals of rapture.

"Live egg hatch?" Higgins asked.

"Live egg hatch!"

"Brontosaurus?"

"Brontosaurus!" Jacob smiled. He squealed. He raised his hands above his head like he had won a prize.

Crowded into the rear corner of the yard, atop pine needles and pollen cones, stood three miniature brontosauruses, each about twelve inches tall, dark brown and slightly iridescent, shining like oily little mud puddles. They bleated like lambs in eerie unison.

The scruff on Bronto's neck stood up as he approached the little dinosaurs with canine caution. He craned his head toward the dinos, inching his nose closer for an olfactory inspection. The little dinos reached their necks forward and met Bronto's sniffing directly, and the four touched noses in a momentary huddle, like a team coming together before a play.

Bronto's little tail started wagging back and forth, and so did the dinos'. Bronto barked once and the little dinos bleated back. Bronto took off running across the yard, and the tiny brontosauruses followed behind in a scuttling pack, surprisingly nimble despite their recent hatching.

Meanwhile Jacob never stopped laughing and squealing. He started clapping when the little dinos took off running behind Bronto, and chased after them himself. Eventually Bronto began chasing Jacob, with the little dino pack following Bronto, and of course Jacob following the dinos. They spent many minutes chasing each other in circles around the backyard. Finally Jacob stopped running and looked at his father.

"Thanks, dad. Brontosaurus." Jacob smiled.

Higgins felt a jolt of something in his chest, a surge of pride zapping life back into the numb collection of muscle tissue formerly known as his heart.

Within a month the little sauropods towered over Bronto. With their long necks they stood as tall as Jacob, but still Bronto was the top dog, the one in charge. The dinos proved gentle and affectionate, rubbing their heads up against Higgins and Jacob, nuzzling in like cats. They romped across the lawn like typical baby animals exploring the coordination of their limbs. Higgins thought they would be lumbering and plodding, their enormity causing them to move in slow motion and shake the ground with each step. Instead they were nimble and athletic, jumping and running with the dexterity of a horse or antelope. They began developing plumage, a fine, yellow fuzz that grew fuller and more vibrant with each day. They seemed happy consuming rabbit pellets and grazing on the lawn, and every day Jacob's spoken vocabulary grew more expansive and impressive, growing just as fast as these creatures hatched from the strange marriage of genetic engineering and tabloid classifieds.

To Higgins the dinos looked identical, but Jacob learned to discern their uniqueness and provided them names. Bolstered by his expanding vocabulary he named them Pop-Tart, Macaroni, and Potato. They eventually added monikers to describe each one's personality — Pop-Tart the shy, Macaroni the loving, and Potato the brave.

Those first two months were magical. Every day the dinosaurs grew a little more, and so did Jacob. Higgins wondered if the dinosaurs were imaginary, or if it might just be a long, complicated dream. When would the dream end?

The trouble started with a broken latch on the dinos' makeshift pen. They wandered out because they were hungry, their growing appetites sending them in search of more and more food. They had stripped the plum and apple trees completely, and trimmed the giant oak as far as their long slender necks would reach. They didn't like pine needles and the turf and rabbit pellets weren't enough anymore. Potato had reached for the blooms of the neighbor's rose bushes and leaned too hard into the fence, sending it toppling like a pile of toothpicks. Before long all three wandered into Mrs. Maccabee's garden as if it were a salad bar buffet.

Mrs. Maccabee was washing dishes and looking out toward her garden, and almost fainted when she saw her prize peonies and roses getting gobbled up by monsters. After she caught her breath she dialed 911. The operator wasn't sure whether to inform animal control or the police, so she called both just to be safe. The call from the police dispatch got picked up by a local news crew that used a scanner to gather leads on slow news days. The *News7* News Van was the first to arrive on the scene, and they were already readying their equipment when the deputy pulled up.

But Higgins knew none of this. He had slumped out of bed and stepped to his window, hoping to see his wife like he did every morning. What a surprise to see the *News7* News Van and sheriff's patrol car blocking his driveway. He saw his neighbor, upset and serious and standing on her porch in a flowery apron. She waved at the deputy to get his attention. The deputy waved back at the woman, which upset her even more.

"Deputy, I got a monster in my garden eating my peonies."

Outside the *News7* News Van, a cameraman balanced a large camera on his shoulder while reporter Dan Dandy straightened his tie and cleaned his teeth with a finger. Hearing the woman's plea they looked at each other, and the cameraman started shooting. Higgins got an empty feeling in his gut and decided he better go out to the backyard and investigate.

Higgins discovered the open pen and followed the trail of bare vegetation to the hole in the fence. Pop-Tart and Macaroni lingered near the opening, and the path of destruction lead him deep into Mrs. Maccabee's garden.

"No Potato, no!" Jacob said. Bronto barked and ran in circles, nipping at Potato's front toes, trying to herd him back home. Perturbed, Potato reared up on his back legs and let out a roar like an angry sheep.

Mrs. Maccabee and her entourage appeared in the back doorway. "See, I told you there was a monster," she said.

"Mary Mother of," said the deputy, stepping onto the rear porch. He pulled his gun and pointed it at Potato, trembling like he had never fired it before. Still standing upright with his front legs flexed slightly outward, it looked like the deputy was getting ready to arrest the dinosaur.

An animal control agent walked up behind the deputy, holding what looked like a large butterfly net. The patch on his shirt read Troy. "Holy shit, is that a dinosaur?"

"I don't know, Troy. I thought you were the expert."

"Well, deputy, aren't you going to do something?" Mrs. Maccabee asked.

"I got some tranquilizer darts in my truck," Troy said, and he hustled off to retrieve them.

Higgins felt sluggish from lack of coffee, and paralyzed by the velocity of events and the chaotic blossoming of thoughts in his head. What legal ramifications were involved in the ownership of dinosaurs? Were they livestock or exotic pets? Was the neighborhood zoned for sauropods? Could dinosaurs be considered assets, and could this impact his home owners' insurance?

More importantly, would this incident affect the ICHE's view of proper homeschooling curriculum? And who had registered that complaint with the ICHE in the first place? He imagined his wife and Marcy were in cahoots, hiding in the bushes together, snapping photos and documenting child neglect. Higgins knew that one of these days he would look into his driveway and see Lulu standing there like a sad apparition of past failures. With his son's help he finally realized that they didn't need her after all. Higgins just wanted a chance at closure, a chance to tell her they didn't need her. He didn't need her.

Meanwhile, Jacob approached the deputy with his hands up like he was surrendering, and for a moment it appeared both Jacob and the dinosaur were getting arrested. That was when the cameraman arrived, live broadcasting the entire scene to the viewers of the *News7 Wake Up Ketchum* show.

"Mister policeman," Jacob said, "don't hurt Potato."

Jacob then proceeded to direct Potato through a series of maneuvers with the confidence of a seasoned animal trainer, starting with a 180-degree twirl while still balanced on his back legs. Jacob used hand motions, a twirl of his finger, a clawing motion, a repeated pointing gesture toward the hole in the fence. Jacob was, after all, a master in the art of nonverbal communication. Bronto tried to help out by barking and nipping at Potato's tail. Together they had him sauntering back toward home in no time.

"Well, I'll be a monkey's uncle," the deputy said, putting his gun away.

"What did I miss?" asked Troy, holding a large plastic tackle box.

"We have just witnessed something remarkable, folks," Dan Dandy reported.

Mrs. Maccabee just fanned herself on the back porch and didn't say anything.

Jacob approached his father, flashing a smile and shrugging his shoulders. Higgins held up his fist and the two shared a bump. Higgins couldn't speak, so proud of his son in that moment his speech centers felt overwhelmed. Luckily Higgins didn't have a clue about how quickly his life would change, with the viral YouTube video, the *Good Morning America* interview, and the endless calls pouring in from scientists, movie producers, and various legal entities. Instead he had this silent, peaceful moment to enjoy to himself, his pride swelling to proportions beyond any attempts of verbalization. Some feelings were so big they couldn't be placed into words. Sometimes when he felt this way Higgins wondered if autism was contagious.

Before crossing the threshold to join Macaroni and Pop-Tart, Potato reached back to grab one last snack for the road, a large, perfectly sculpted rose that could have won a blue ribbon at the county fair. Having witnessed the final indignity she could stand, Mrs. Maccabee fainted, but the deputy was able to catch her before she hit the deck.

The cameraman followed Potato back to the fence line, finding Higgins standing there dumbfounded in his house slippers and bathrobe. He hadn't shaved in days, and his robe had no belt or fastener around the middle, revealing a chasm of bony, white chest and black hair descending to striped boxers.

"Excuse me sir, can you explain what we just saw?" Dan Dandy stepped toward Higgins with his microphone.

The cameraman pressed forward also, pinning Higgins against a rose bush, which caught hold of his robe, tugging on the fabric and biting into his skin.

Higgins pulled his robe a little tighter and looked into the camera, clearing his throat. How could he possibly sum up the emotion, surprise, and pride he felt? He took a deep breath.

"Brontosaurus."

THE FIRST LAST MERMAID PORN QUEEN
Yvonne Yu

1

licks her fingers and tastes herself. The taste is as salty as you might imagine but not fishy, not in the least. It lingers in the mouth like well-aged vinegar. This is one of many unknown things about the world's only (to the best of her knowledge!) mermaid porn queen.

2

smiles as the blonde bronze human swallows and tells her, *This is my first time. I mean, not my* first *time, but my first time doing* this. She strokes the side of his face like a mother and tells him it is easier than he thinks, that the motions and mechanics are mostly the same, that he just needs to spread his legs a little wider to make room for the end flaps of her tail. *I don't want to hurt you,* he says. *It's okay, I'll tell you if you are,* she says. And then they do things that no mother should ever do with their child, and it doesn't hurt or even seem awkward, really, and afterwards the mermaid porn queen feeds him some smoked kelp she had prepared as a snack.

3

already knows what you want to ask her. Yes, she has a vagina, or at least an opening that could be considered one; no, her tail does not split in two like legs to expose it. Under her navel, on the ventral plane of her tail, a patch of smoother flesh leads into a gentle slit where penetration can occur. Her tail itself is a taut length of muscle, and can be flexed to open herself up to different positions.

The parts of her that could potentially house life do not fall on the human spectrum, so she has no need for birth control. She has ovaries but not the corpus luteum of the female mammal, which secretes hormones necessary to the maintenance of human pregnancy. If she wanted a child, which she does not, she supposes she would deposit her unfertilized eggs out in the water and find a mer-mate to ejaculate over them. It is not currently known if this would work with human males, or if it did, what the resultant conjunction would look like: would it divide in perfect fractions, becoming one-fourth fish and three-fourths human? Would it be outwardly all man, but soft-spined on the inside, unable to hold itself up above the density of the water?

These are questions that are easier not to ask. She has seen human children before, splashing in the low surf, and feels nothing but a mild sympathy when they discover the harsh sting of salt in their eyes.

4

is a diligent worker. She does not drink on the job nor will she accept one without a contract, dated and laminated so she can keep a copy in her files beneath the sea. Any film crew she signs with must operate by strict ethical standards, including full consent and bargaining power for performers. She negotiates for combs, for French face creams, for DVDs. She is particularly fond of *Young Frankenstein.*

The mermaid porn queen is a good businesswoman, so good that sometimes the set crew forget she is a porn star and fall in love with her slick straight back. They vie to be the ones to rearrange her tail in between takes, or to spritz her down with a light oil-water mixture (for rehydrating, and to add a sexual glisten to the skin). But at the end of the shoot they always slink home to look for girls who have never bared their breasts in 4K high definition at a 19:10 aspect ratio.

She doesn't mind at all. It's their loss, really.

5

knows that one good thing about having a tail in this industry is never having to put up with the language she sees mapped onto other women's bodies. The one director who dared refer to her "va-jay-jay" was quickly removed of that tendency; being the only mermaid porn star and therefore a limited commodity affords her a relative degree of power. The mermaid porn queen knows her sex is not a flower or a pussy but a three-dimensional location that beats and breathes and consumes with ravenous delight. Because no one quite knows what to call it they switch from saying *Your cunt tastes amazing* to *You taste amazing*. This makes the mermaid porn queen purr with pride; it is she who moves her body, it is she who deserves the crown.

6

has been known to take lovers, too, although she is clear that she does not mix work with pleasure. There are not many mer-men in the sea, and even less who deign to swim where the humans gather, so more often than not she tends to take up with the human kind. She takes them into the water and kisses their hipbones, lets her long hair hover in clouds around their naked bodies.

Sometimes she bares her teeth very close to their faces and flares her gills like fans on the sides of her neck, pretends she is about to bite into them. The way their eyes widen, as if all the legends of sirens and sea witches were true, makes her laugh so hard she almost forgets to let them up for air.

7

pulls her jaw open in front of a pane of polished sea glass until the corners begin to ache. Then she holds her lips apart until the whole structure of her face turns numb. It is becoming increasingly popular for directors to start their films with a close up of her performing oral sex, the screen tight on her head and back, then petering back to reveal the sudden curve of her skin into scale. From those first frames, they tell her excitedly, no one ever knows the difference.

She sloughs dull scales off of her tail and shakes it out to its full length. That difference, she thinks, is in pretty damn good condition for its age. Honestly.

8

uses the rough edges of seashells to file down her nails before lesbian scenes. By now she must have done over a hundred of them.

When girls are first sent to her, they don't know if they should treat her as female or fish. She does not swagger like the men they are used to but she still takes up space. In the beginning they stick mainly to her breasts, her neck, they supply shy kisses like new lovers. In return she teaches them how to dip their fingers to give her pleasure; she wraps her tail around their fine waists to offer support as they lean in to her touch. Some girls ask, after the shooting, if they can take a closer look. They peer into her body with unabashed curiosity, sanitized stares, keeping a careful distance as if these parts are now entirely new. As if what they'd just done was have sex with their eyes closed, with their mouths open, drinking in the core sensations but not their surroundings.

9

reads her latest fan mail, which is left bi-weekly under the southernmost rock on her shore. A man who runs an art collective expresses his deep respect and awe for the breadth of work she has committed herself to. He wishes to invite her to dinner (an indoor tank can be provided, of course) and requests she call him names while she sticks a kebab skewer up his ass. The mermaid porn queen pens a polite decline, which includes a cautionary line about hazardous materials for anal insertions.

10

is showered with semen for the last time in the day. The milky globules preserve most of their form where they land on her scales, glittering there like scattered pearls. Look at what you did, the mermaid porn queen laughs, lifting her tail to hold the jewels to her co-star's eyes. He laughs too, penis beginning to droop comically to his thighs. When the final cut comes out, it will not include this scene; the way human and mermaid grin at each other over their ridiculous, beautiful intimacy.

The first and last mermaid porn queen watches the human dry translucently on her skin. *I am a work of art*, she tells herself, pulling the waterproof microphone wire from her back. *I am a job well done.*

BAZAAR
Y.t. Sumner

I DIDN'T REALLY THINK IT THROUGH.

Not really. I just swallowed as many of Mum's sleeping pills as I could and lay down on the couch.

I bet they did one of those huge assemblies at school where the girls who called me a slut cried and hugged each other and the teachers handed out pamphlets on teen suicide prevention. I bet Trish Baker with her bruises and junkie dad wished she had the guts to do it too.

It doesn't matter now that I'm here. Like most things I did when I was alive, I kind of regret not thinking it through. Like having sex with Trish's dad. It wasn't so great but it was better than nothing. If I was religious I probably would of thought I would go to Hell because of all the guys I fucked. But I'm not religious. I kind of wavered in that grey shade of not thinking about it like most people I knew. I didn't expect this.

There was a moment, though, that made it almost worth it. There was no white light or spooky tunnels. Just the deepest sleep I'd ever had. It was like sleeping for the first time. Like all those other times had been practice to get to this real moment of sleep.

And then I woke up.

I finished all of my stories in English class with that. Every single one would have that last line. Mrs. Payne would make us read them out in class and when I read mine and got closer to the end kids would start to giggle. My mouth dried up and the words cracked my lips but I kept going. Mrs. Payne always wrote nice things on the stories I handed in and so for her I kept reading. Until I looked up and saw her laughing behind her hand.

I was surprised to see her here the other day. She looked older than I remembered and her throat had a bruise around it I'd seen on others here. She was browsing through a vintage broche section across from my stall. She was holding the pins to her chest and sticking it out a little to see in the mirror. She looked like a chicken. I remembered she had a kid with leukemia and that she left the school to look after him.

She looked up from her pin clasped to her chest as if she could faintly hear the memory too and looked right at me.

It's a shame to see you at the Bazaar, Deanna.

I tried not to look at her purple throat.

Same, I guess.

She put down the broche and came over to my stall.

You have some beautiful dresses here.

I looked at the rack of theatre costumes. They were all labeled from the plays they were from.

Do you want one?

She recoiled and said that wasn't the way it worked.

I wanted to ask her what I was supposed to do but instead I blurted out something worse.

Is your son here too? Because I'm kind of hoping to see my Dad.

She stepped back towards me.

Deanna, I'm sorry about that time I laughed.

I said it was all right, but thought, why do people always say sorry when it's too late?

Then I realized what she meant.

My Dad isn't here is he?

She shook her head and teared up as she told me this place was just for us and then walked away in proper tears. I guess her son wasn't here either.

I didn't move from my stall. I decided I wasn't going to believe her and then I saw the boy I lost my virginity to. Jay did it in his family pool three years ago, just after Dad's car accident.

The amount of people I knew here was making me nervous. Jay used to write morbid poetry about death. He told me after we did it that life would never measure up. I didn't listen at the time. He was always saying weird shit and I was too focused on how gross and painful the sex had been.

When he passed my stall I wanted to take his hand and touch his pale blue face. I wanted to tell him I finally got it.

But I didn't.

I hid behind the rack of costumes from a production of *A Streetcar Named Desire*, I hid and watched him pass and knew I was even more of a coward here than I was in life.

I spent the days sorting through the jewelry and the nights rearranging the costumes. Every time I thought about going out into the Bazaar it made my heart beat like crazy. And that was stupid, my heart had stopped in the ambulance on the way to the hospital but I had my fingers pressed to my throat trying to feel the rhythm when two little girls walked in to my stall. Blue dresses, ribbons in blonde hair. They even had black Mary Jane shoes.

One of them picked up a little ceramic horse I hadn't noticed. As soon as she touched it the words leapfrogged from my mouth.

Be careful!

She didn't look at me and I cleared my throat.

It's delicate. You'd hate to break him, right?

The girls shrugged together and she put the horse back on the ledge in an offhand way. They both stared at my wrists and the horse grabber asked why my wounds were closed.

I looked at my arms and thought it wouldn't be proper to tell children about the times I tried before so I told them they were from a long time ago.

We did it in the lake.

I felt my phantom heart almost stop at the singsong unison of their speech.

When Mum and Dad divorced they said they would take one of us each. The water hurt our chests but it was better than being split up.

I wasn't sure what to say. I felt as if I should somehow cover their shame and so I asked if they'd like a blanket, because I hadn't noticed it before, but their dresses were wet and smelled musty, like wet clothes left in the washing machine.

They said no and left the stall, but one of them turned and said I shouldn't worry about the horses because everything here was already broken.

I walked over to the shelf and saw the horse's mane had broken off. I sat down in the stall and made a little bed out of Blanche Dubois' dress. I curled up and wondered if Trish's dad thought that I did it because of him. If it was something that made him lose sleep. I wondered if Mrs. Payne still felt bad about laughing at me. I wondered if Mum would end up here too. I snuggled into the dress and thought that was a terrible thing to think.

So I stopped thinking and tried to concentrate on the sound of my stopped heartbeat.

TOGETHER, WE CAN SAVE A LiFE
Christopher Lettera

UNDERSTANDING THAT DESERTED shopping plazas are sometimes cemeteries for Cabbage Patch Kids: that's the first key to letting go. The second is this: John Wayne Carlson was eighteen years old when he told me his plan.

In another week he would have been nineteen. He was going to co-op, not college. Three months studying mechanical engineering at a private school outside of Flint, Michigan, and another three working the floor at a General Motors plant in Mansfield, Ohio. Four years of this set to rinse and repeat and he could have started at seventy grand anywhere in the country.

He had, as we all do, this life.

He'd play shortstop in the summer and fall. On weekends he'd move furniture with his dad at an H&R Block complex downtown. Every day after swim practice we'd smash at Taco Bell. That was where he told me —

"Do the math."

He'd drink the same thing day in and day out. Always a large soda. Always a Baja Blast with lots of ice. Twice that week he'd won a free crunchy taco from the peel-off sticker on his drink and he'd told me, smiling, "Mike, you do this long and often enough and you'll win the million. Buy two large sodas instead of one. Drink what you can and throw away the rest but at least double your chances."

Good-natured, skinny John Wayne.

Two weeks before graduation, a letter printed on thick and coarse cream-colored paper arrived at his house saying he'd won the million. He was going to be flown to California and crowned El Presidente at Taco Bell corporate headquarters, a hulking, labyrinthine tower of mirrored glass and steel where he'd be handed a big floppy check and get photographed by the local news media.

When his mom found him, the blood seeping from underneath his hair had dried and clung-stuck his head to the floor in a dark crimson paste. A small piece of his skull was floating around in the open drain next to the washer and dryer. He hadn't been drinking. He forgot to towel himself off coming out of the shower and cracked his temple falling on the corner of the bottom basement step.

Some of our parents have been laid off. Last week, Gabby Braun's Dalmatian got massacred by a slow-moving tractor-trailer. Shit happens. But really, most of us don't understand the extent to which life in Hubbard, Ohio, is sacrifice to some strange mystery.

Shields Road. The clock on the dash glows 11:15 and the train rushes by against my headlights, carrying the smell of track-rust and pinecones. To the left — inky treeline that stretches out into forever pitch black. To the right — that house. 3359 Nowhere. Abandoned and alone under the mile-long shadow of the woods, a single porch light blessing chipped siding.

The blinking red of my phone, a text message:

Hal-eh shoma chatoor eh?
(HOW ARE YOU?)

"It's not always like this," Chad says.

"Sometimes a victim places his hand on your sternum, even close to your neck."

Chad is forty and balding and up to his chest in the chlorinated water of the Hubbard indoor pool, teaching us how to save lives. He speaks in measured beats.

"This is out of panic," he says. "Out of fear of drowning and dying."

"You have to be ready for this."

"Remember," he says with a practiced calm. "Together, we can save a life."

This is the motto of the Red Cross, printed in tall black letters on wallet-ready paper cards that prove certification in LIFEGUARD TRAINING AND FIRST AID and CPR/AED FOR THE PROFESSIONAL RESCUER. Earn one and you're licensed to save a human life.

There's five in this class, among us a fifteen year-old girl who plans to guard at a country club and a retired optometrist whose wife passed in her sleep.

"She just went one afternoon," he tells our lot.

When we're finished in the water we climb out and circle around a life-size, shirtless rubber dummy with bulging fake nipples and a hideously frozen smile.

"Michael, come over here and help me please," Chad says.

"Okay."

"Put your hands on the dummy's chest."

"Okay."

"Do you feel his heart? Do you feel the life left in the dummy?"

"Yes."

Always, lying in bed, there's the shriek of the train whistle in my mind, and later — louder — the silence of 3359 Nowhere standing against the woods. Born and raised in Hubbard and I've never noticed that house. Now three nights coming back from the pool and 3359 aches by the tracks, looming, and there's the desire to get out and go inside, to touch the walls and to walk on the floor, if there even is one.

CPR. Cardiopulmonary resuscitation. For cardiac emergencies. To be employed until more advanced medical personnel arrive. Thirty compressions and two breaths for an adult, child, or infant. To resuscitate them. To bring them back to life.

I repeat this over and over in my head: a mantra, a whisper to pray me to sleep.

"Do you feel it?" Rob asks.

"No."

It is the sinking feeling in the pit of your stomach. *It* is the corner of Liberty Plaza.

"I mean, who knows what kind of shit they had going on back there that night?" he says. "Christ, could have been demons and shit, man."

Rob owns a brown S-10. The front cab is clean as a whistle. Spotless and lemon-scented. Pop open the back and you're liable to vomit in Technicolor. All across the truck bed there's a gruel of salt and cement dust and layered spots of something red and sticky. Rob's dad runs the local Culligan water supply store. Old ladies order salt for their water softener systems, Rob delivers it in 60-pound bags in his S-10. When he's not working Culligan, when he's not laying concrete sidewalks for port authority at the town airbase, he hunts small game and skins it right out of the truck bed on a blue tarpaulin he says used to be his baby blanket.

In high school he wrestled at 152. He's 190 now, a national qualifier in Olympic-style lifting. Tonight we're sitting in the deserted, vacant parking lot of an abandoned K-Mart shopping center chasing a sickness we both felt in our guts two months ago as we sat in the S-10, our eyes wide, our souls paralyzed.

"I mean, I know *that* feeling," he says. "That fucking panic of throwing 120 kilos over your head and thinking you're going to drop it on yourself. The fear of blowing out your knees. Scott, my lifting partner, he did that. He held his dislocated kneecap in his hand for a half hour before the paramedics came. Screamed like a bitch too, but don't tell him I said that."

"All that," Rob says, "was nothing compared to that night and that feeling."

He's rarely so eloquent. Two months ago we were driving out of Liberty Plaza, a rotten gathering of crumbling stores spread across an empty, weed-ridden lot. We came upon a corner, a little enclave where a dozen or so tiny shops might have thrived before everything shut down. In this space: a headless Cabbage Patch doll, an overturned shopping buggy, a plastic bag floating mid-air against moon-glow, graffiti ("Satan knows").

"I'm telling you," Rob says, "Something bad was back there."

He shines his brights against the greasy windows on the front of the old K-Mart, on what ten years ago might have been the entrance to an automotive section that offered cheap oil changes and vending machine Kit Kats.

"See that? Zombie hobos could slam up against those windows right now and I wouldn't budge. Rabid plague motherfuckers. But whatever was in that corner was bad. If you let your mind take a walk in places like that," Rob says, "you might get fucked up."

I'M GOOD, YOU?

I text back in English a full day later.

E Street Radio is all Bruce Springsteen. Twenty-four hours a day. When they're not playing his records they're playing interviews and he talks about dreams and why he made *Nebraska*. For six years, it's been the cracked and dusty voice of Bruce Springsteen telling me everything's going to be all right, everything's going to be ok.

I burned Grace a copy of *Darkness* but she never quite understood.

She's an Air Force linguist now. Persian-Farsi. She spent last summer in the desert with her face wrapped in tight black up to her soft blue eyes. She picture-mailed me her military ID card once. In the tiny text she's 5'6" and 120 lbs. In the tiny photo she's country-plain and beautiful, a rural school runaway with hair long and brown and a face that can save.

"You're afraid of things leaving," she said as she packed her bedroom into boxes.

"You're afraid of things changing," she said after her graduation from Basic in San Antonio, Texas.

There's two disposable cameras worth of glossy pictures taken at Lackland Air Force Base stuffed in my top dresser drawer. Five pictures of me and Grace. Forty-five of cloud stalled in Lone Star sky.

The Hubbard BAILEY'S HOMEMADE — once a veteran's hall — is now an ice cream shop. The new VFW opened next to the library and has MEMBER'S ONLY stickered across the front door in big-print camo lettering. The girls at Bailey's wear unflattering bow-ties and black aprons and never look as happy as something like Rainbow Rock-Pop sounds.

"What are you getting?" Rob had asked John Wayne.

"Cotton Candy Explosion."

"What the fuck is that shit?"

"Cotton candy ice cream with sprinkled rock pops."

"You fairy."

"What are you getting?"

"Pink Champagne sherbet."

"Hi," this girl says behind the counter.

Homeless Steve in the parking lot of St. Pat's in Hubbard swears by the numinous feeling. "The numinous feeling," he chortles, "is that moment of realization, of truth, of recognizing something beautiful and the validation of self that comes with it." Homeless Steve will shake your hand after services and say, "Peace be with you."

"That is the most wonderful feeling of awe," he assures. "That is the most numinous of feelings."

That was GRACE (her nametag silver and bright).

"Fuck me sideways with a wrench."

"Nice. Fuck me sideways with a tractor blade."

"Fuck me sideways with a toothbrush."

"Gross," Rob says. "And not painful enough."

How we got into Pauline's Lounge across the PA line was Rob and I both grew patchy beards. 10:35 and he's put away six Millers against my carefully paced two. Robert James Godfrey seems placid but I can just imagine the alcohol coursing through his muscle mass.

"I'm Mallory!" a woman shouts.

She gulps a two-dollar shot of Black Velvet and sneezes. She's pretty but she's either twenty-five or she's forty and in the dim light I do not know.

"Where do you go to school?" she asks.

"Hogwarts."

"What?"

"I said I'm eighteen, Mallory. My best friend just broke his head and died in his mom and dad's unfinished basement. I have two hundred dollars in my savings account. Last night I sat in the dark and listened to *The Ghost of Tom Joad* on cassette. I'm on hiatus from fun. Do you understand, Mallory?"

"I went to Kent State!" she hollers.

Fuck me sideways with a roaring chainsaw.

The muddied slab of carpet in the doorway, the RC Cola pop machine from the early 80s, the stacks of Rotary flyers — everything about Hubbard Community Pool reeks of chlorine. Class by class, it becomes second in familiarity only to oxygen.

In the front office, chlorine mingles with mall-bought perfume. There's Krystal with a K on a swivel chair, her leg balanced on a metallic filing cabinet as she paints her nails a sour, glaring purple.

"You're late. How come?"

"The highway's jammed with broken heroes on a last chance power drive."

"What?"

"Nothing. Nevermind"

"I'm really sorry about John Wayne," she says.

"Me too."

"Chad is on deck with the brick. He says you need to shower before you get in the pool. You have to swim your five hundred first and then he'll sign you out after you dive for the brick in the deep end. Oh, and you can't be in here."

"Sorry."

"Staff only in the office. But happy early birthday."

"Thanks."

The men's room hasn't changed in the last twenty years. Navy blue lockers. Sky-blue tile on the shower floors. The toilets are teal. In the ladies', everything is pink. I took swim lessons here before I could read and wandered into the wrong locker room by mistake.

My dad would take me when I was three and four. When I got tired, when the muscles in my legs would cramp up and I couldn't kick anymore, he'd say –

"Swim to the other side. You can make it."

Last night, Rob had the windows down in the S-10. We're leaving a steak restaurant and there's this scream, this all-at-once exclamation of surprise and panic and I say –

"Rob, slow down."

"Why?"

"I said slow the fuck down. Those people might need help."

There's a woman in her eighties splayed on the asphalt. She's staring upward. At streetlights. At cloud loping across night sky. On her face — a half smile. In her eyes — a glistening. Her cheeks are garish red and her wig is noticeably slipping off her skull. A man — her husband, maybe — kneels beside her, his hand placed on her forehead, his lips mouthing "Everything's going to be all right, everything's going to be okay."

A woman in an over-sized hoodie bolts out of her SUV. There's kids in the back windows, their faces and hands pressed up against the glass. She's skittering, patting her mouth with her hands, her voice cracking as she says over and over –

"We called 911. We called 911. We called 911."

"Michael."

"Yeah."

"Michael?"

"What?"

"Wake now. Go down there and rescue that brick."

"Okay."

Underwater. A waking, translucent death. The sinking away from reality.

3359 Nowhere. One night you'll get out of your car and go into that house.

Twelve feet under. The tough skin of my heels hitting the grimy pool bottom. No air. The weight of the brick. Fifty pounds of rubber. A human life in my hands that I'm supposed to drag to the surface and breathe back to life.

You'll get out of your car and walk towards that house not out of choice but necessity.

The tightening of my lungs.

Out of reasoning real and clear only to you.

I imagine their inward collapse and, for a moment, a suffocating panic.

Inside 3359 there's darkness, metal and broken plastic, and a realization, a truth.

The surface. Shimmering and crystalline. The feeling of emptying out. The absence of heart, of heartbeat.

There's a smell rank and foul like dried piss and old paint and there's a sound, a faint and approaching noise like the crackling of footsteps in the hall.

Maybe it's nothing. Maybe it's everything.

GODZiLLA READiNG HAiKU
Christopher DeWan

"ARE YOU GONNA EAT THOSE?" He was eying up my pancakes.

"Of course I'm going to eat them. I wouldn't have ordered them if I wasn't going to eat them."

"Oh. I just thought maybe you weren't going to eat all of them."

No way was I going to eat all of my pancakes, but no way was I going to share them with him, either. "You want me to get the waitress, so you can order your own pancakes?"

"No, that's okay. I'm not that hungry."

The trouble with Godzilla is he's always hungry. And he breaks things by accident. And he scares people. It's kind of a drag.

"Here." I cut my pancakes down the middle. "Take half."

"You gonna eat that sausage?"

"You wanna come up?" I ask my girlfriend on the stoop.

She nibbles gently at my ear. "Dunno. Is your roommate home?"

My roommate, Godzilla, is home. I play with the button on my girlfriend's shirt but don't answer.

"I think I'm just gonna go home," she says.

The alarm clock goes off and I stumble out of bed toward the bathroom. I pass Godzilla, coming out. "Don't go in there!" he warns.

And he's used up all the toilet paper.

"Sorry!"

Sometimes we sit in our apartment in the dark, in the quiet, though it never gets completely dark or completely quiet because Tokyo leaks in through the windows. The lights flicker off the walls, and horns bleat, and sirens, and sometimes through acoustical miracles, conversations carry up from the street to our window. But things feel mostly muted and far away, and it's relaxing. We enjoy it when we can afford to.

Godzilla has a little plastic lamp clamped to the cover of the book he's reading.

"'Summer grasses — all that remains of soldiers' dreams.'"

"That's a good one," I say.

"Sad, right?"

"And not sad, too. Just, you know, true."

He's got little Post-It notes sticking out of his favorite pages, and he turns to another: "'Clouds — a chance to dodge moon-viewing.'"

"Ha," I laugh.

"Yeah," he says. "Yeah…"

"Okay, one more."

He flips pages. "Here's one." He clears his big throat. "'Not one traveler braves this road — autumn night.'"

"Hmm. I don't know about that one."

"I like it because it's quiet," Godzilla says.

I nod. "I get that," I tell him.

"What did you do today?" I ask Godzilla as he walks in the door. But he shrugs and looks at me kind of sheepishly and lumbers off to his room, and I decide it's probably best if I don't watch the news tonight.

"What's it like?" I ask him once. "All the killing." He frowns at me and looks like he wants to spit, and I'm sorry I asked. He absent-mindedly picks up our salt shaker and crushes it and then looks embarrassed.

"It's not like that," he finally answers. "The guy who gets off on destruction, on being big and strong and powerful — I'm not that guy."

"I know you're not that guy."

"It's lonely being a monster."

"I guess it probably is."

"I'm glad you're my friend," he tells me, and I hug him the best I can with my little arms and his big body, a real hug, tight, so he knows I mean it.

GiRL EATEN BY A TREE
LiZ KiCaK

Mark Ryden: Oil on Canvas, 2006

So sweet! Like peach nectar. Even her
bobby socks tasted like candy.

Strolling among whispery pines, larkspur
and honey-scented clover. A trio of skipping girls never suspected
that innocuous alcove in the oak, where robins fought
to lay their eggs, would soon be stuffed with one of them.

He was ravenous — starving, rooted in place.
He never hesitated to wrap his branches
around her slight waist and shovel her in
his open mouth. She flailed and kicked
but he ate her headfirst so the screaming was brief.

Her golden ringlets tickled the top of his throat.
He gagged and almost spit her out but then he got a taste
of the candied flesh. His bark breaking into her body — the joy
of the feast surpassing his best epicurean dreams.

Her shoulders, still in their blue silk frock,
slid down with ease. Each pearl button of her dress
gliding over his tongue. The slight puff of her belly,
her syrupy hips and thighs — thighs soaked
in peach nectar, soaked in maple sap!

At last, he is sated,
drowsy — not the least bit sorry.
Her doe-eyed, porcelain friends stagger away
with the buckles from her maryjanes.

UNEXPECTING
Anna Lea Jancewicz

(for David (not Lee Roth))

FINALLY, ONE AFTERNOON, in a fit of desperation, you fish one of Husband's plain white undershirts out of the Semi-Clean Pile and with a Sharpie make a custom maternity shirt.

I'm not just getting fatter, ok? There's another human in here.

Husband says you shouldn't count your chicken before it's hatched. And in fact, when folks begin to ask *What are you hoping for?* you find yourself replying *A human.* Husband prefers *We're hoping it'll be Asian. Asian babies are really hip now.* He also lets them know, in a confidential tone, that werewolf does run in his family. *On my father's side* he whispers, sotto voce. You think this may be true.

Husband proposes naming the baby *David Lee Roth, Jr.* You make a counter offer. *Only if we can go with Anna Lita Ford, should it be a girl.* Stalemate.

You love *Fern.* Also, *Opal.* Husband decrees: *No naming babies after plants or rocks. Why beat around the bush? You may as well name the kid Bongwater.* You scowl.

Ulcer Hellhammer, Husband says, beaming. *That's gender neutral.* You agree to disagree. *What about Agony Hellhammer?* he asks. *Is that more girly?*

This baby will be Irish <u>and</u> Jewish, he says, *You know that means it'll have a tail <u>and</u> horns.* You add to the gift registry: lots of little kilts, lots of little hats.

You attend childbirth classes, the kind where the instructor wears a large pendant around her neck that resembles the Venus of Willendorf. She plays tranquil New Age flute music at the end of each session, and urges you to visualize rainbows and waterfalls. Husband elbows you as you both sit cross-legged on the floor and whispers *I think I have dog crap on the bottom of my boot.* You smell this to be true. You both agree you are out of your element.

You decide to just have the baby in your own bathtub. Your birth plan goes something like: "Play *Whole Lotta Love* on repeat, very loudly, and yell *fuck* a lot at the top of my lungs until we see a head." Amazingly, this works really well, and none of the neighbors call the cops. Husband says *Led Zeppelin is for queers and losers.* You're the one who is shitting a broadsword, so he can eat it. But you love him so much more now, somehow.

The baby has no Asian features, of course. And surprisingly, no horns *or* tail. You do note upon waking, after the first postnatal full moon, that your wee darling is spattered with a fair amount of blood, chicken feathers stuck to rosy cheeks. Ulcer Hellhammer is still the cutest baby you've ever seen. It's true. She really is.

ONLY ONE GOOD REASON
TO GET A HAIRCUT
Sloan Thomas

TRYING TO OUTRUN MY PROBLEMS in a rusted 1972 Chevy Nova takes more than an eighth of a tank of gas.

There is only one gas station in town. It's next to the junkyard on the other side of the bridge. The bridge is currently blocked. The bridge is blocked, because the owner of the junkyard died — leaving behind a shed stacked with dynamite.

The amount of time it will take tribal police to remove the danger is up for debate. So I don't let my car idle. I sit at a full stop with like fifteen other cars. May sits beside me. We're waiting for explosions... and gas too.

Lately I think about cutting my hair — cutting it real short, spiking it up. May says there is only one good reason for an Indian to cut her hair. She's right, but maybe I'm tired of looking like her. Looking like me. When we fight, which isn't much, she braids our hair together. We walk around connected, but mostly we just smoke pot. Lots of pot.

That's what we're doing right now. May steals weed from her mom who sells it to tourists looking to worship ancient trees and mythical Indians. Her mom knows we steal it. May's mom beats her for the missing weed. I tell her, better to get beat than ignored. Sometimes she agrees.

I can't remember the last time my father asked me where I've been. Mostly he's drunk. Mostly he misses his wife. Mostly I just see his callused feet sticking out the edge of his bed, but only when the bedroom door's cracked. Occasionally women come over. They toddle and trip into my father's room. In the morning they edge and slink their way out. They always forget to close the door behind them. *What are you born in a barn.*

I steal my father's keys. May shows up before I can leave. She shows up covered in dirt. It's crusted in her eyes, clogging her ears, falling off her like fat raindrops. Tears run down her face and I mix them with the dirt. It makes a mud mask softening her skin, hiding her scars. She tells me about the party, about the boy who tried to smother her in the dirt. She says, "I'm soiled."

We take side roads and back ways and expand the distance. We never make it past the bridge.

May likes to hot box the car, fill it up with smoke. But the sun is beating down on us and we have to open the windows. Because the widows are open, Wolfies steals our joint. His hand snakes in through the driver's side.

I'm related to Wolfies. Everybody is related to Wolfies. Nobody knows where he lives. If you ask Wolfies how old he is, he'll tell you, "My birthday was yesterday, but you can buy me a present tomorrow." If you're missing something there's a fifty percent chance Wolfies took it, and if you pay him there is a hundred percent chance he'll find it. Wolfies is like your favorite curse word — you only use his name when something bad happens, but man do you love to say it.

"I'm taking this as payment," he tells me.

"What have you found?" I ask him. He takes his time — smokes the joint — dances back when I try to grab it. I watch him scrape the embers across the asphalt and throw the roach in his basket. His basket is full of slippery eels... and other payments.

"You know the 2,000 pounds of dynamite downtown?"

I think it's more like fifty, but Wolfies has never been one to be bogged down by facts, and I've never been one to stop a good rumor. I roll my eyes and tell him everyone's already heard that.

Wolfies smiles, shows his teeth and whispers, "It's not the dynamite I'm telling you about."

I know and maybe May knows too, because she stops rolling the joint in her hand, that Wolfies isn't just telling a story and we aren't just sitting here and everything isn't just a coincidence.

"They found bones. Bones under the dynamite."

I don't move. Wolfies digs in his basket. I know what he's getting. May starts looking for the sack of weed we keep hidden for emergencies. I hold her hand. I hold her still.

She knows, just like I know, like everyone knows — when you ask Wolfies to find something you have to settle your debts. You have to settle your debts with what you promised.

I can smell the eels on the metal. May holds my hand or maybe I'm still holding hers. I remember my mother brushing my hair, braiding it up. "Never cut your hair," she would tell me. "Always braid it tight." And I never cut my hair. I always braid it tight. But I know the price for calling Coyote — even if it's to find your mother — even if she's only bones under dynamite. I can feel the scissors on the back of my neck. There is only one good reason for an Indian to cut her hair. I'm a good Indian.

JOLLY ROGER
Michael Sions

THERE IS A DEAD BODY IN MY BASEMENT. At least I think it is dead, but I have not checked for a pulse, so it could just be sleeping every time I go down there. It has been there since the day that I found it there and I have not moved it since that day. I thought I should move it out, but instead I kept it, just in case I ever needed it.

☠☠☠

It has been there, in my basement, for a long time now, but I still have not moved it. Sometimes I go downstairs to get something and it is there, because dead bodies stay in the same place if no one moves them. I wonder if it will talk to me, but it never does. It just sits there, not moving, and not talking either. By this point I know it is dead and not sleeping, because it has started to decompose.

☠☠☠

An insurance salesman comes to my door to try to sell me insurance. He knocks once, but I do not hear it, so he knocks again. This time I hear his knock, and I answer the door.

"Hello," he says.

"Hi," I say back.

"How about I sell you some flood insurance for a real dandy price?" he asks, in a southern accent.

"Why do I need flood insurance?" I ask back, without an accent.

"Well," he says, "this house you got here's real near a floodplain, and so you're at risk of a flood."

I still do not know what a floodplain is, but I know that I should, so I just nod and he keeps talking.

"If a flood were to come in right now," he talks, "then you'd lose everything you got stored up in this real nice basement I see the hatch for."

I tell him that I do not have very much in my basement except for a dead body that I found down there.

"You have a corpse in your basement?" he asks. He looks horrified.

"Yes I do," I say back, "do you?" He still looks horrified.

"Why, n-no. No I certainly do not," he says.

"Well," I say back, "then I have more dead bodies than you do."

☠☠☠

I am at a yard sale that my neighbor is having, and I am buying a picture of cats playing Scrabble. I tell him that I wish I had a cat to play Scrabble with, because all I have is a dead body in my basement, and I don't think it knows the rules to Scrabble.

My neighbor tells me that cats do not know how to play Scrabble, but it is a shame that I only have one dead body in my basement. He tells me that he has five dead bodies in his attic, and he calls them corpses.

I remember that the insurance salesman called it a corpse too, instead of a dead body. I decide to start calling mine a corpse, but I do not move it to the attic, because the attic is already mostly full.

☠☠☠

I am out jogging when I see a man who lives down the street walking his dog. He tells me that he is glad to see me keeping healthy, because healthy people make better leaders.

I tell him that I am not a leader, and he tells me that I should try running for office, because I have a strong build, and people like their leaders to have charismatic skeletons. I ask him what a charismatic skeleton might look like, because I used to have a corpse in my basement, but now that it has been decomposing for a while it is mostly a skeleton, and I would like to know if I have a charismatic one. He tells me that he does not think that having two charismatic skeletons will be better than one.

"But," he says, "you should put it in your closet. All the good politicians have a skeleton in their closet."

☠☠☠

The insurance salesman is back at my door.

"Hello," he says again, "how about I sell you some tornado insurance at a dandy price?"

I ask him if my house is on a tornado plain too, and he says no, so I ask him why I should buy tornado insurance.

"Because," he says, "since we last talked, I've collected six dead bodies, and, now that I have more of them than you, you should listen to me when I tell you things, and I'm telling you this: you need to be ready for a tornado."

I am now ready for a tornado.

☠☠☠

I am trying to sell my house so that I can move into an apartment, because my house is too big for just me to live in. There is a young couple inside my living room, and they ask me why it is they should buy my house and not any of the other houses.

"You should buy this house," I tell them, "because it is the only house on the market with a skeleton in the closet." I do not know if this is true, but my neighbor is not selling his house so I think that it is.

"That's horrible!" they say. They tell me that they would not want to buy a house if there was a skeleton in the closet. I tell them that that is good, because I was probably going to take the skeleton with me when I moved out anyway. They ask me if this is an area prone to natural disasters, and I tell them that it is near a flood plain, but it is not in a tornado plain.

"Oh, good," says the wife, "I'm terribly afraid of tornados."

They do not buy my house, because they want to buy a different one. Instead I sell my house to a family of four whose kids are named Chad and Robert. Chad and Robert want to see the skeleton, but their parents tell me to take it with me. I take it with me when I move, but there is not a closet for me to put it in so I just put it in the living room.

☠☠☠

I have met two of my new neighbors. One of them is a pirate, and the other one is a first grade teacher named Renee. Renee is very fond of her dog, and so I tell her that I have a skeleton in my living room if her dog wants a bone. She asks me if I can get one right now, so I bring her back a bone.

Her dog loves the bone, and so later she asks me for another bone. I bone her three times before I tell her that I cannot give her any more bones, because my skeleton is starting not to look like a skeleton anymore. She tells me that if I do not have a full skeleton, the next best thing is a skull and crossbones, so I should keep boning her until I only have the skull and two other bones. I do it, and I put the skull and crossbones on the counter.

☠☠☠

The insurance salesman is at my new door. I do not know how he found me again.

"Howdy," he says, "how about I sell you some greyhound insurance at a dandy price?"

I tell him that I do not live in a greyhound plain, and I have never heard of insurance for greyhounds.

"Well," he says, "say a greyhound comes in and messes up all your stuff. Well then, if that happens, we cover it!"

I ask him what he thinks the chances are that a greyhound would be able to break into my apartment and mess up all my stuff. He tells me that if I do not buy his insurance, it is almost certain that a greyhound will come in and mess up all my stuff, but if I buy his insurance, then it probably will not happen.

I am no longer insured for tornados, but I am quite prepared for greyhounds.

☠☠☠

I have the pirate over for dinner, and he sees my skull and crossbones.

"Arrrrrrrrrr," he says, "that be quite a jolly roger ye got there." I tell him that I didn't know his name was Roger, and I ask him why Roger is so jolly.

But he just says "arrrrrrrr" again and changes the subject.

☠☠☠

I run into my old neighbor at the grocery store, because my new apartment is not very far from my old house. I ask him how the five dead bodies in his attic are doing.

"Not so good," he tells me. "The cops are investigating things and it's only a matter of time before they start sniffing around too much and figure me out. How'd you get away with it?" he asks.

"Get away with what?" I ask.

He tells me that I am clever and he winks at me.

Later that day I hear sirens.

☠☠☠

When I come home from the grocery store I find my door open, and all of my stuff messed up. I look at my skull and crossbones and both bones are gone, so I go to Renee. Her dog has one of the bones, but the other one is nowhere to be found.

"Say, what breed is your dog?" I ask her.

She tells me that he is a golden retriever.

WHERE'S THE BEST BBQ IN THIS TOWN?
Matthew Myers

OOO-HOO. OH MAN OH MAN OH MAN. You really want the best? This is what you have to do: Make sure you have plenty of cash. They don't take credit cards or any of that. What hotel are you staying at? Okay, head south from there, go two miles down whatever road that is, two blocks past the third gas station. There's a little shack of a place with bars over the windows and all the lights out. Park in the back near the pile of old Christmas trees. Watch your step. The asphalt's like waves. If you become disoriented, look up and try to find familiar stars through the sodium lights. There will be nothing but a swirl of yellow-glazed bugs. Despair and then strengthen yourself. Let the shivers run down your spine and out like gutter water.

Knock on the door marked DELIVERIES. Use your knuckles. Don't use the palm of your hand. Knock three times, each one louder than the last. Don't knock again. Don't doubt that you knocked right. You did just fine, just fine. Make sure your shoelaces are tied. Be on guard. There are killers and thieves in the shadows of the laundromat across the lot. They will strike if they feel you're not on point. They may strike anyway, so keep your wits a-fucking-bout you.

A woman will answer the door. She'll ask you if you need to talk to Arturo. Don't answer. After the silence becomes unbearable, she will ask you if you have a reservation. Say Yes. You won't, but say Yes anyway. She'll ask your name. Say 'Frankfurt Burns, party of two.' Make sure you have two in your party. Say you're Rich's other nephew and cough twice into your fist. Don't forgot to mention that you're Rich's *other* nephew or she'll become suspicious. Technicolor spiders will appear on her shoulders and you won't know whether you're awake or dreaming, and you may forget your mother's maiden name.

She will open the door and hand you a manila envelope. Accept it immediately. In the envelope will be a map and a postcard with a picture of a horse on it. On the back will be a number written in pencil. Memorize this number. Say 'Thank You, Sharon.' She will crinkle her eyes as if her name is not Sharon. But it is.

Return to your car. Pray no dogs come out, but do not pray out loud. Watch your corners. Make sure no one's in your back seat before you open the door. Drive back to the gas station. Fill up your tank and buy a two-gallon container. Fill that as well. Turn off your headlights and flip the map upside down. Follow it to the letter. The drive will be long, and you will abandon hope of ever reaching your destination. Keep going. You can't fail. Your appetite is on your side.

The moon will appear to pixelate and shudder. Night clouds will turn blood red and take on a horrific majesty. Suicidal ideations may take hold, and your steering will pull left a bit. If you're a praying man, pray. If you're not, don't. Hold fast and breathe slowly into your hunger.

In your rear view the road will chase you. You will know sorrow and you will know fear. Your bones will make sounds that your ears will doubt. You will come to the end of the map and still you'll see nothing but corn, and the howls of animals will remind you of past loves. Don't ignore the rush of nostalgia. Feel it fully, cry until you're dry, let the memories become small enough to fit into the glove box, then place them there beside the flashlight, the tire gauge and the gun you didn't know was there. If you must doze, doze. The rumble strips will bring you back.

Press the radio on and scan the AM band until you hear something like the laughter of children. Signal right but turn left and drive until the laughter dies. Pull over and kill the engine. Leave your keys in. Get out of the car, take three deep breaths and follow the sound of footsteps through the kicked-up cloud of gravel dust. Feel free to fear, but don't doubt the maker of the footsteps. Just follow and keep your own thoughts hidden from you.

A screen door will find you like a spider web in the dark. You're here. Squeak the screen door alive and open. The cicadas won't be there to cheer you on any longer. Step inside and go blind from the neon light of beer signs. When your eyes tune in, your Hostess will be standing there. Her hair is a black majesty. The scar on her forehead will do nothing to hide her beauty but don't gaze too long or she will own your soul and the pink slip to your car. She will take your coats and offer you salvation. Let your face fall down into her breasts without embarrassment. She will hide you and heal you. There is a blue rose tattoo on her collarbone. Count the petals. This will come in handy in future lives. The number on the coat check ticket will feel strangely damning.

Hand her the postcard and tell her your number from the postcard. It's no longer written there, but you remember it, don't you? Of course you do. Follow her into the dining room and when she offers you a seat, ask her for another; for a booth, closer to the window. She will try to talk you out of it. Do not, for Christ's sake, let her talk you out of it.

Your Waitress will come by about a half hour later. You'll think it's Sharon but it's not. You'll then think it must be her twin sister, but Sharon has no twin. She'll ask if you want the buffet. There is no buffet. Say No. She'll ask if you want to hear the Specials. There are no Specials, but don't, *Do Not*, let her know that you know this. When you're very sure she's done with the Specials, say you'd like to see the Tuesday menu, unless it actually is Tuesday, in which case simply ask for 'The Menu.'

A doughy-faced man at the next table will grab your shirtsleeve and ask how's the weather in El Paso. If you happen to be from El Paso and have only left recently, feel free to tell him, but use plain English and avoid meteorological jargon (this will enrage him and you'll have to fight him to first blood in the parking lot with silverware and jumper cables and you will lose). Otherwise, laugh like it's an old joke and say, 'Oh no, I'm not that easy,' then give a little laugh, then he will laugh too and slowly release his grip from your sleeve, leaving a runish mark that you will ponder in your old age when all of your friends have died.

Study the menu. The words will spin slow and settle onto the page and into the sauce-smeared fingerprints of past diners. The fingerprints are mysteriously, Pygmi-ish small. The jukebox will cue up Walter Pitchfork's *Pigfucker Lacrimosa No. 4* and it will make you fear for the lives of your children. Especially if you have no children. Resist the urge to call and check on them or all will be lost. Concentrate hard on the menu. There is a troubling wisdom in the description of sauces if you're the kind who can find it.

Now order.

This is your time. Do not falter. Easy now.

The Burnt Tips are gone by the time you get there. Don't even ask. The Pickled Sow Cunt is what the place is known for. Order it with beans and slaw or not at all. The Pulled Pork Platter has tons more meat then the Sandwich but costs the same. The Chicken is just okay, but if you're a chicken guy, I guess you'll like it just fine. The Ribs are excellent, but they've been known to induce temporary blindness in whites and Chinese. Small price to pay, some say, but know the odds. They only do full racks, no halves, and don't even think about splitting it with your partner because fingers are lost that way more often than they're not. The Devil's Cock-n'-Balls is exactly what it sounds like. *Do not* order this unless you literally want to eat the Devil's cock and balls.

The 66-n'-6 Sampler is the way to go. I always get the ol' 66-n'-6. It of course comes with the Devil's Cock-n'-Balls, but just let them lie there if that's not something you feel comfortable digesting.

The needle will mysteriously jump from *Pigfucker Lacrimosa No. 4* three bars from the end, and either *Whammy Bar Mama* or Slaughter-house Kate's *Cuntrag Blues* will come on. They have identical guitar solos but are otherwise nothing alike in sound, substance or mettle.

The sauce cart will sidle up hot and loud and Gravy-Face Gary will ask you what sauce you fucking want in a voice that brings to light all of your father's infidelities. There's Miner's Lung No. 6, Death Throes Rose, Bonnie's Special Red, Ragwater No. 5 and Bonnie's Xtra Special Red. If you're braving the Devil's Cock-n'-Balls, I'd use the Xtra Special Red and man oh man let it flow. Otherwise you can't go wrong with the Special Red. Miner's Lung is an acquired taste but if you're like me, you should always be acquiring more tastes, right? Ragwater No. 5 doesn't hold a candle to Ragwater No. 4 but that recipe died violently with its progenitor Polly 'Pretty Please' McGuillicutty at a Greyhound station in Joplin. Death Throes Rose gives me fevers and the shits so I rarely touch the stuff.

The bathroom is to the right of the aquarium. Don't mind the chickens hanging from the Bible-blackness of the drop-ceiling grid with no drop-ceiling tiles. Those are just the Voodoo chickens. The chickens they use for cooking are in the mop closet, which is inspected quarterly in accordance with local bylaws, so breathe clear and easy.

When you exit the bathroom, mind the Irish wolfhound chained up to the slop sink. He doesn't bite or leg-hump, but lose yourself in his gaze and you risk a hellish vision quest, suspended in a mist between two waxing crescent moons, descending into a bright blue madness, remembering all pre-verbal pains and soul scars, before reemerging awash in glory fire and a new soul-skin, released from his spell and placed safely back in your seat by the mighty oaken arms of Gravy-Face Gary, also in accordance with local bylaws. Also, the Wolfhound will own the pink slip to your car (if you've already lost this to the Hostess, you're fucked, brother).

If you're lucky, your food will be waiting for you when you come back.

Enjoy your food and eat sloooow. Chew each bite thirty-seven times or the chef's allowed to leave a trace of his soul in it (again: local bylaws). Chef's a decent guy but I wouldn't want a goddamn mote of his soul in my belly, and I eat most anything.

Now when you're done, and if you still own the pink slip to your car, pull out and drive in an easterly fashion with the headlights off until you hit the main road. Take nothing but lefts until you're back on the highway. If you sweat something that doesn't smell like your own sweat, don't worry, that's situation normal. Ignore the sounds of hooves clopping beside you. Now suck on that starlight mint and let that toothpick do its work and drive, drive, drive.

And of course there's Porkin' Mama's just two blocks that way. They're pretty good too.

WE LEFT HiM WiTH THE DRAGGiNG MAN
GRaHaM TUGWeLL

BLOOD.

Bright where the shaft of sun falls on it.

Dark in corners where the flies gather.

Gristling every surface, fat waxy beads of flesh and blood, stickiness dripping on slender threads…

We stand in the doorway.

Bodies have come to pieces in here.

We can smell them.

Taste them.

In the doorway we stand, boys shocked and wordless.

In the dark before us something moves —

"Help."

Speaking with a weak and broken voice —

"Help me."

Barely there at all…

"Please. Help me."

Four boys, running across a field as fast as their bodies will let them —

Cormac Sulltry, short and stout, covers ground with a speed that belies his size, vaulting the low slant-angled fence he hits the corrugated earth; staggering, stiff-legged, for a step, the impact knocking the hat from his head.

It lies upturned, unheeded on clay — Sulltry stares at a horizon hammering up and down with footfalls, arms like pistons, breaths shredding between grimacing teeth.

Saltsweat pinches eyelids.

Nothing will slow him.

Boots thump the dirt behind, flattening the hat like a careless pet — Kevin Shields — huge, unmolded, left hand on right shoulder tight, trying to keep the blood within. A rose is blossoming under his fingers, turning the green of his jersey brown.

Curly hair bouncing, jug ears bright red, Kevin hollers through crooked teeth "Cormac! Cormac! Cormac! Cormac!"

Nothing will convince Sulltry to turn, to look back.

Close behind, in the wake of Shield's ungainly frame I run.

I've lost a shoe to the lip of the ditch and a stitch is folding the breath out of me. Slapping a palm to settle my glasses, I leave a smudge across one lens, blurring the backs of the boys. My other hand plunges in pockets —

My inhaler —

Where's my inhaler —

Left it behind —

With —

There's a screech behind me.

Little Tommy Sweetnam, foot swallowed by a rabbit hole, pitches forward, heels of his hands and knees hitting the turf, shrill screams bursting his hamster's cheeks — "No! Don't leave me!"

Can't catch my breath — pins in the heart of me —

Cormac a distant smudge, Kevin loping after him, and Tommy struggling, blonde head pressed to the mud —

I take the softness of his hand, drag him to his feet. "We left him," says Tommy, tears carving pink in the muck. "We just left him."

I grab him by the sleeve and haul him over the tumbled fence.

And the last of us, the fifth boy —

Alby Gorman.

Where's Alby Gorman?

We left him with the Dragging Man.

The five of us were friends because no-one else would have us.

Cormac Sulltry was bossy and arrogant and short-tempered and always convinced he was in the right. He wore a cap, like a gang leader in his comics.

Kevin Shields was slow and his father was strange and his mother took a knife to her wrists a month before school began.

Tommy Sweetnam was soft and gentle, and while all the rest of us were growing up, he remained a baby, younger than us in every way.

And me, stricken with pneumonia at an early age and never truly recovered; a sickly air hung round me, made me cold and distant. Happy to wait and listen.

And Alby Gorman…

Was Alby Gorman.

We came together, the scraps and odds and ends…

Friends because no-one else would have us.

We learned that Cormac was fearless and cunning and clever and Kevin was kind and loyal and loved his kittens, and Tommy was an artist, such a voice—he'd sing for us, behind the Water Tower. He was good like that.

And me, I'd listen.

I was there for them.

Even Alby Gorman.

Screams.

Bringing children around corners, pressing teachers against windows, sending Joe the caretaker racing across the tarmac.

Tommy finds me by the rosebushes.

"He's doing it," he stammers, pudgy face pale, "Doing it again!"

Leaving my lunch on the wall I run, up the slope, along prefabs to the gravel behind the boiler, pushing through gathered children — Cormac and Kevin already there.

So is Alby Gorman.

Kneeling on the small of Pascal Givens' back, one hand worked entwining in his hair, Alby presses the trapped boy's head down amongst the sharp and scraping stones.

Givens' voice — the high shriek of a pet crushed in a closing door: "Help me help me help me —"

No-one moves.

Because the look on Alby Gorman's face — that placid concentration, the tongue-tip in the corner of his mouth. Softly, serenely, he twists Pascal Givens' arm — eyes bulging pale bubbles, close to popping, free hand slapping and clawing gravel — Pascal can do nothing as Alby drags the limb around and up the length of his back.

It resists.

For a moment.

We all hear it—

The soft wet click of something forced out of place.

Pascal's scream rises until, at the edge of hearing, it empties him. Still he lies on gravel.

Only then does Alby Gorman look at his audience.

Cormac impassive and Kevin sick and Tommy distraught: "Why Alby?"

Alby looks at us as if the answer's obvious, as if we're stupid. He smiles. Says "I wanted to see his new watch."

(The limp wrist, red and purple, and the yellow plastic of a strap)

Alby Gorman shrugs. "He wouldn't let me. So I made him."

Joe the caretaker lifts the boy from the gravel, pushes his way through the children.

Alby's smile widens. "What's the problem? I didn't take it."

Joe puts Pascal on the backseat of his car.

A curve of kids and teachers stare down at Alby Gorman.

Wondering what he is capable of.

What he will do next.

Alby Gorman squats on haunches.

"It didn't land on his feet."

He prods the white kitten.

"I thought they always landed on their feet..."

He rises as Kevin gathers the limp thing in his hands — his silent tears huge and bright and awful.

"Maybe I kicked it too hard," says Alby Gorman and he grins. "Give me another one, Kevin. Let's try again."

"How high can you sing, Tommy?"

They sit behind the Water Tower, watching traffic pass.

Tommy plucks at his sleeve.

"Em," he says, "Em. Dunno."

"Try, for me," says Alby Gorman.

"What, em... what song do you want, Alby?"

He smiles.

"Surprise me."

"This is… em… this is something Mammy and her sisters sing."

"Come and look out through the window."

"That big old moon is shining down…"

Alby nods. "Can you go higher?"

Tommy's voice sharpens:

"Tell me now, don't it remind you."

"Higher."

And sharpens further, hangs there, shivering:

"Of a… blanket… on the… ground."

"Let me help," says Alby Gorman.

Hands close on Tommy's throat.

Tighter and tighter.

Until song becomes scream.

Alby Gorman.

Brown haired and blue-eyed.

And all of us so scared of him.

He lived with his grandmother and little sister until, one day, he lived with just his grandmother.

And he smiled.

All the time he smiled and stared and we learned that life was easier when he got his own way.

The four of us, we became friends because no-one else would have us.

But we weren't friends with Alby Gorman.

He didn't know the meaning of the word.

Once, he found me by the rosebushes. Sat beside me.

I settled my glasses. "Are you okay, Alby?"

He ran his finger over thorns. Snapped a budding rose from its stem.

His voice was low. "Why are they scared of me?"

Stomach a cold plunge, I replied, "Who, Alby?"

He plucked a curved leaf, flicked it in the air.

"The rest of the class."

Another red leaf fell.

"The people who say they're my friends."

Scraps of rose settled on his lap.

His blue eyes did not blink.

"You," he said.

Wanted to run. Could feel my chest collapsing—fingers searched for my inhaler.

Finally, I found my voice. "You... you hurt people," I whispered. "You don't know how strong you are."

"And when you hurt them..."

"You don't care."

He smiled.

Horrible.

"I hurt people?" he said.

I nodded.

"Is that so..?"

My inhaler — where —

He tapped his lap.

Curls of soft red plucked from the bulb...

I stared at them.

"Eat them."

Unblinking.

"Eat... them..."

His hands curled in fists.

Imminent things.

Breath dragging, throat and neck enclosing, I bent. With numb lips, plucked a leaf from the lap of Alby Gorman.

Chewed.

Swallowed.

I sat back.

He smiled, patted my cheek.

"We're friends. We're kind to each other. We play games."

His fingers rested for a long time.

"Don't be scared of me. I don't want that."

He left.

The taste.

The taste of roses.

"No more," says Cormac Sulltry. "Something has to be done."

He slams his fist into the palm of his hand, the way they do it on TV.

We're in Tommy's house, in his bedroom.

Kevin sits on the floor, Tommy and I sit on his bed.

Cormac strides, repeating, "Something has to be done," under his hat he scratches his greasy scalp.

"But what?"

Silence falls.

It is Kevin who solves our problem.

"I know a place," he says, running fingers along his kitten's ears. "Dad... tells me... The place where he and Mam went. A terrible place. There's a thing inside it."

His voice drops to a whisper.

"The Dragging Man. That's what she called it. It had its hold on her and wouldn't let go. Dragging her into the dark. It has no hands and no feet but it holds you tight. In the end she had to cut herself away..."

Kevin looks at the biscuit-coloured kitten in his lap. Patches mews and plays with his fingertips. "We can leave Alby with the Dragging Man."

Cormac has that look. A plan, falling softly into place. He replaces his hat.

"Yes," he says.

That half-away look, working the angles...

"Yes."

Deciding the way the world will work...

"But we all have to agree," says Cormac Sulltry. "All of us."

"Yes," says Kevin without hesitation.

"Yes," I say, after a moment.

Tommy rests his head on folded arms.

"I can't."

He shakes as tears come through him.

"It's not right."

Cormac looks at me and nods his head.

I put my hand on Tommy's arm.

"Tommy," I say, "He hurts people. Someone has to do something. Before something awful happens."

Tommy shakes his head.

"You know he has it in him."

I touch the bruises on his neck.

"Why us?" sobs Tommy.

"Because we're his friends," I say. "He trusts us."

Tommy looks at me. "Do you think we should?"

I nod.

Tommy drags a rattling breath and tries a little smile.

"Okay," he says.

And the door opens.

Alby Gorman.

Looking in.

Brown-haired, blue-eyed and smiling.

Tommy gasps. Kevin clutches his kitten. It hisses.

"Secret meeting?" whispers Alby. "Was I not invited?"

He taps the wood of the door.

We say nothing.

"Why not? Am I not your friend?"

Cormac clears his throat.

He has a plan.

Always.

"We're planning a camping trip, Alby. It was going to be a surprise."

Alby grins. Something glistening on a surgical glove.

"Count me in."

Down we go by Wishing Lane and up into the woods and hills.

Cormac Sulltry leads the way, and Kevin Shields close to guide, next is me and Tommy Sweetnam. Last of all is Alby Gorman, smiling at sunlight through the trees and throwing sticks at birds.

Five boys on a camping trip.

Singing. Laughing. Looking back at Alby Gorman.

Kevin points. There is a house, dark and broken, in the crease where two hills meet.

"Here," says Cormac Sulltry, "Here's where we camp."

And Kevin stares at the door ajar and the black windows and we must call his name three times.

Slowly, and slanting, the tent goes up.

(Why straighten it? It won't be slept in.)

We watch Alby Gorman wander up the overgrown path.

He presses his face against dirty glass, runs his fingers along the splintered wood — a piece comes away with a crack. He turns, his grin the gleam of a freshly-dropped turd.

"Dump." He skips the wood back down the path. "What do you think happened here?"

Kevin makes a strange sound, deep in the back of his throat and Cormac coughs to cover —

"Alby," he says, "Let's explore." A single bead of sweat crystals his brow. "Let's explore."

Alby Gorman looks at us and our stomachs freeze over. Time turns to creaking slowness. After an age Alby puts his shoulder to the door and shunts recalcitrant wood aside.

Cormac and I follow him, Tommy a pace behind, and Kevin staying where he is.

We go in and find:

Filth and broken furniture and stained rags on the floor, a fireplace clogged with leaves, and a cracked mirror returning our shadowed faces in pieces. Peeling wallpaper. Swollen wood. A shaft of sun trapping a zithering fly.

And there is the smell of beer, sharp and bloated, making our heads swim.

And there is something in the darkness beyond.

Moving slowly through the other rooms.

I look at Cormac, my chest a pinched unbreathing.

He nods.

And the thing we've come to find leaves the darkness for the light. It passes the doorway and stands there, looking out at us.

Pink.

Wet.

Ribbed.

A worm, trying its best to be a man.

It has no feet.

It has no hands.

Its arms and legs go on and on.

The Dragging Man.

"Children," it says. "Stay with me. Stay with me."

Alby Gorman's smile disappears.

For the first time there's a look —

Confusion. Almost… almost… panic —

"What..?" he mumbles.

"Now!" cries Cormac Sulltry.

We grab and we push.

We are not strong — Alby Gorman will not be moved —

"Children," cries the Dragging Man. "Stay with me. In the dark."

And there's a scream —

Not the Dragging Man.

Not Alby Gorman.

Kevin Shields, thundering down the path, bursting through the doorway, screaming: "You kicked them — kicked to pieces —"

He grabs Alby Gorman and with his strength added to ours we force Alby further in, dirt and rags entwining in our feet. It dawns on him: "Leaving me — trying to leave me here!" and Alby Gorman fights us, pushes us back —

I trip on the broken sill of the door.

Five boys falling, tumbling into summer suns but Kevin is not quick enough — Alby Gorman digs his nails into his chest, feet scrabbling for purchase on the tall boy's thighs.

Kevin screeches "Get him off me! Get him off! Aaargh!"

Cormac and me, we take Alby by the arms and try to pull him from Kevin — Alby's teeth close upon the meat of his shoulder and when finally we manage to wrench him off a long wet string comes away in his mouth.

The soft wet noise of it…

Blood gushes and Kevin collapses and Tommy is softly sick through threaded fingers.

"Cormac!" screams Kevin, hands flapping at wounds down neck and shoulder, "Cormac!"

"Not my idea," mumbles Tommy, "Not my idea…"

And as Alby readies himself to pounce again, as the Dragging Man drifts through the room, I see…

There is a stout branch in the grass by the front door. I pick it up and break it across the forehead of Alby Gorman.

His eyes roll up in his head.

"Ulm…" he says, gulping, "Ulm…"

He steps backwards, puts his hand upon the blood licking over an eyebrow.

Without a sound the handless arms of the Dragging Man close over his throat, over his chest and it is almost a loving thing.

Alby Gorman is dragged into the dark.

Slowly the door of the broken house closes.

We stand there, looking at that door, for a very long time.

"Pack up," says Cormac sharply. "Pack up and home."

Kevin makes a noise. "Cormac, it's not stopping. I can't..." He paws at the wound. "It won't stop."

"No," weeps Tommy Sweetnam, his head in his hands. "No."

"Hurry," shouts Cormac Sulltry

We busy ourselves.

There are noises.

We try to ignore them.

Hammering.

Bodies falling.

Short gasps and sighs and grunts and once, a long, resounding scream.

And there are shadows behind the dirty windows....

Tommy Sweetnam —

We are busy. Before we can stop him he is down the path. He is through the door.

Tommy Sweetnam —

He was good like that.

"Alby — Alby," he cries, "I'm sorry — I'm sorry —"

We are behind him shouting, reaching out to pull him back — but we are too late.

We enter the house again.

Blood.

Bright where sun falls on it.

Dark in corners where the flies gather.

We stand in the doorway, shocked and wordless.

A body has come to pieces.

Something moves —

"Help."

Speaks with a weak and broken voice...

"Help me."

Barely there at all...

"Please. Help me."

We look down at the twisted thing cowering in the corner.

"He got out," whispers the Dragging Man, staring with his one remaining eye, "Couldn't hold him. Help me…"

The bruises.

The bite marks.

The severed limbs.

"Run," says Cormac Sulltry.

Four boys, running as fast as they can across the field.

And where's the fifth boy?

Where's Alby Gorman?

We find out, one by one.

Cormac, by knife, in the carpark.

Slashes on his palms and chest.

He fought.

July 26th.

Kevin, at the foot of the garden, black bruises on his throat.

The last straw for his father.

The kittens left to starve.

August 5th.

Tommy, in his bed, a pillow over his face.

So small and delicate.

You'd think he was asleep.

August 17th.

And me?

I wait now for Alby Gorman.

And what words will we exchange, before…?

I wait.

Remembering four boys running across a field, as fast as their bodies will let them.

Remembering the taste of roses.

Seeing a body disappearing into dark.

We were young.

We were scared.

We left him with the Dragging Man.

ABOUT THE HiDiNG
OF BURiED TREASURE
KiMbERLY LOJEWSKi

IT'S COMMON ENOUGH to hear about the finding of buried treasure, but the real trick is in the hiding. The finding is easy. You just need some head lanterns, a pick axe, an old sea-worn map, waterproof matches, and a rune decoder. Possibly some dynamite and trip wire if you are being shadowed. But hiding it, that is another story. It is a lifelong toil. And trading doubloons in this economy is almost more trouble than it is worth sometimes. Don't even get me started on grapefruit-sized emeralds and rubies. Vials of diamond dust are sure to raise an eyebrow or two.

Our island is chock full of treasure. It is bursting at the seams with plunder and booty, trap doors, trick caves, and rocks marked with big mossy X's. Pop has trained Jezebel and I to keep it hidden. We scrub the X's off the rocks, cover hidden entrances with branches and hornets' nests, and fill up the sunken mounds of old pirate graves until the earth is smooth. In the winters, when the ground is frozen, and the waves are funnels of salt ice, we practice ice surfing in crowns and tiaras, check our booby traps to make sure they are not frosted over, and search the island for new treasure. It's just us and the polar bears. We throw secret carnivals and glittering parades.

In the summer, there is no time to play. We are positively swarmed with visitors. People come here from all over, although most of them don't know why. Their free-market noses are trained to follow the scent of wealth across oceans and deserts. It is the real story of humanity. They smile at us and sniff the air curiously. They look around at the tangled trees and spur-filled sands and try to come up with convincing explanations for their visits.

"We just had to come see your charming island," they say.

Or, "We felt some draw to explore this part of the world."

They can feel the ground wealth-trembling, even though we tell them that it is just the shifting of tectonic plates and the rumblings of a resident live volcano.

Jezebel and I take great care to appear slow and backwards. We can wear as many crowns and tiaras as we want in our wintry solitude, but when there are visitors on the island, Pop likes us to seem dim-witted. Jezebel paints her lips in uneven red circles and kinks her orange hair with boxes of out-of-date home perms. She talks with a slow southern drawl that has no place on a windswept northern island, but no one ever notices it's farcical. Jezebel likes to experiment with new guises. She's a few years older than I am.

I keep a standard profile. I spin an old yoyo from one finger and blow giant circles of bubble gum that burst on my cheeks. I never wash my hands or comb my hair. Pop grins at them from the docks, big holes in his teeth where he yanked them out with a socket wrench. He's got a set of whale-bone pirate falsies, chipped from chewing on gold coins, that he wears when we go into town to trade.

Pop isn't our real Pop, and Jezebel isn't my real sister, but we feel like a family just the same. Pop stole us from a mainland orphanage and raised us up to be his pretend children. He plans to leave this island's legacy to us one day and retire to the Caribbean. Somewhere that isn't quite so hard to keep a secret all the time, and somewhere he can hear the whales sing while he sleeps. Of course, all that changes the day that the summer winds blow a hot air balloon our way.

I first see it while I am up in the lookout tower. Summer winds are never any good here. They always seem to blow things straight towards us. The winter winds blow things away.

The balloon is a big one, a fancy one. It is shaped like a medieval castle, with elaborate, brightly colored turrets and banners flapping about in the sky. Whoever is inside it clearly does not know how to fly. I watch it swoop and bump across the breeze in crazy circles for a while, until eventually it trumpets in defeat and wedges itself into the spiky branches of one of our bramble trees, a good twenty feet up from the ground. The nylon shell of the balloon shreds into cheerful confetti, while the thick gushing flame singes the leaves and sends the island's wombat-sized, golden-eyed sea gulls flying up into the air with loud caws.

It has happened before. That is half the reason the bramble trees are there in the first place. We don't like folks getting too good of an aerial view of our island.

I watch the man inside try to work out a way down for a while before I get bored and wander off. There is a boatload of people arriving at Dead Man's Cove and I scamper over there to make sure that everything looks just the way it should: inhospitable and ugly. We arrange bleached whale bones in the sand and throw laxative-laced fish guts on the rocks every day, so that our ravenous monster birds will shit all over them while swooping and dive bombing their picnic lunches of wine and marmalade sandwiches.

After a few minutes of deflecting curious questions with a surly scowl, and refusing to carry anyone's bags or help high-heeled ladies across the sand, I forget all about the treed man inside his castle of a hot air balloon. There are plenty of greedy ground people around to discourage and dismay.

"Charlie," Jezebel whispers to me from behind a thorn bush. She is dressed like a pygmy today. Her orange hair is coated in mud and she has war paint drawn on her face. "Did you see the balloon in the trees?"

I nod. "He's stuck good. No getting out for a while."

"The colors," Jezebel says. "I've never seen anything like them."

She looks slightly bedazzled. I draw her attention to a couple of backpackers sharing a bag of granola and looking hardy and determined.

"There's no zip lining here," I call out to them. "No waterfall jumping. No rock climbing. No hang gliding, No swimming with dolphins. Just hungry bears and giant seagulls. If you get back in your kayaks and head south you'll find an island with rainforests and elephants."

They eye me up suspiciously, wander around a little until their waterproofed boots are caked in excrement and fish guts, and then rinse themselves off and head back out to sea. One of our polar bears ambles out of the trees and sends the remaining tourists screaming for their vessels.

"That's an easy day's work," I say to Jezebel, tossing the bear some silver herring from my backpack. But when I turn around the bushes are empty and my sister has disappeared.

Jezebel is breathless over dinner. She is humming with excitement, some secret girl-ness that I cannot understand. Pop doesn't notice. He sucks the meat out of crab legs, crushing the hard shells with his jaws. Butter and boiled seawater drip down his chin. Every now and again he breaks the silence to mutter something about bloody tourists, or the plummeting price of jewel encrusted crowns. Jezebel sighs into her dinner plate. It looks like she is sculpting balloon castles out of her potatoes.

That night she has a headache so I am on treasure duty on my own.

"Sorry, Charlie," she says, scrunching lines into her forehead. I can tell she's faking. I have spent my entire life reading her expressions. "I don't feel very well. I won't be any good trying to cave climb or check traps tonight."

It is the first of many solitary wanderings.

The man stays up in his basket all summer. He makes a rope ladder he can crawl down from to go fishing and swim in the ocean. At night he seems perfectly content to sit in the wicker basket, cook fish and grill star fruit over the open flame, and count stars through the wispy tatters of his balloon. He has no sense of urgency. He doesn't seem to be trying to get anywhere. Pop doesn't like him too much.

"Simpleton," he says, watching him from a pair of binoculars. But he doesn't pay him much more attention than that, though one night he does have me make a honey trail to the tree to try to attract the bears. Sometimes we have to do this sort of thing.

It's mostly the other people that are the problem. They consume our entire summers. They arrive in ocean liners and jet planes, sometimes helicopters that drop parachuting squirrel gliders out over our private land. Once an entire family beached themselves on our island, sun-swollen and half-starved, on a log raft they built themselves. They kissed our cold shores like they had finally come home. They seemed surprised to find it was just sticks and sand. The look in their eyes was heartbreaking. I wanted to drop some jewels in their pockets as they pushed back off to sea, but Pop said no.

"All we need is for one of these vultures to catch onto what we got here and we'll lose everything," he said. His eyes get a little gold crazy when he talks like this. When he really gets going they turn into spinning 14-karat gold wheels.

We do everything that we can think of to throw them off track. Pop plants fields of ragweed, sour grapes, wild garlic, and saw grass. He threads the trees with bramble vines and poisoned thorns. *His* Pop let loose a plague of jumping spiders, giant rats, and polar bears upon our island. Until the rats ate the jumping spiders and the polar bears ate the giant rats. We tried to train the polar bears to guard the treasure caves, but animals have no interest in cold, glittering inanimate hordes. We keep them around anyway since they hypnotize the tourists with their moony pelts and silver fangs. They gobble them up from time to time, but it still doesn't stop the people from coming.

Ever since the hot air ballooner caught Jezebel's eye something is different with her. I am not a trained treasure hunter for nothing. I tap the walls and floorboards of her room until I find the hollow spot that contains their secret correspondence. It is in a peeling cigar box, buried under a heap of tiaras and jewels. It is full of perfumed letters and declaratives. Lots of "I love you's" and "I want be with you forever's". I try to tell Pop but he can hardly hear anymore after taking so much booby-trap shrapnel in his ears.

"Don't bother me about yer sister's lady problems," he says. He is busy planning out how to rig a decoy island across the bay with fake treasure to distract the gold hunters for a while. This last summer was particularly stressful. One couple with eye-patches and peg-legs put their tent up right across the grass patch that covers the mouth of our underground tunnels. We had to pepper spray the garlicky breeze while they were sleeping to send them coughing and sputtering away.

"Times are getting tough, Charlie," he says. "We gotta buckle down. Reinforce our perimeters. Tell that ducky to quit mooning over hot air balloons, perm her hair up, and help us keep this treasure hidden. That's what family is for."

That isn't what Jezebel thinks anymore. She sits at the desk in her room making kaleidoscopes of gemstone chips and gold dust. In her journal she wrote about plans to sell them in fancy galleries on the mainland. She wants to leave our island.

"Charlie!" she jumps when she sees me standing in the doorway. I have cat-burglar feet. One of her cheeks is shimmering iridescent where she must have touched her face. I scowl at her.

"Jezebel," I say. "You have to forget the man in the balloon."

"What man in the balloon?" she asks, her face turning an unattractive shade of plum. This is the trouble with girls. You can't trust them worth a dime.

"You're leaving us," I say. "Or you want to anyway. What has he said to make you want to abandon me and Pop?"

"Oh, Charlie," she says, and her whole body shudders. "I'm not a kid anymore. I can't stay here forever. This is no kind of life for a woman to have."

With her frizzled hair and muddy clothes, Jezebel looks nothing like a woman to me. I tell her as much and she throws me out of her room with all of the strength of a born-and-bred treasure hider.

"I'm warning you, Charlie!" she yells through the door. I hear the slide of locks and clicks of latches. "Try infiltrating my personal space again and you'll be impaled by an eleventh-century Viking sword!"

This is enough to make me cautious. Jezebel is a booby-trapping master. She loves restoring ancient Scandinavian weapons. I give up on her. Instead I decide to go to the source of the problem: the Lotharian rake in the hot air balloon.

Pop is frying gull eggs in the dark in the kitchen. He's drunk on pirate rum and wearing a long pajama shirt and night vision goggles. Singing a shanty about adventure on the high seas. He doesn't even notice as I slip out the front door, exiting from a concealed fort cover made of sewn up thorn branches and poison berry leaves.

There is a path through the brush to the man's tree. I suspect my sister has carved it out. I tread in her footsteps quietly, so as not to spook any bats or bears or other nocturnal predators. I am almost to the site of their aerial love trysts when I make an amateur's error. I step into a trip-line ankle snare and immediately find myself swinging back and forth upside down, spiky brush snarling in my hair. This is Jezebel's handiwork. No doubt about it. It never occurred to me that she would booby trap the hot-air-balloon man from me and Pop. This thought sends a piercing pain through me even as the blood rushes downwards towards my head.

A treasure hider is never unprepared. I cut myself free with a dagger from my belt and tumble into a pile of thorn bushes, the ensuing howls giving me away completely. The man in the balloon is alerted. By the time I've righted myself he has climbed down his rope ladder and is standing before me.

"Charlie," he says. I have been imagining different versions of the devil himself trying to steal my Jezebel away. This man doesn't look anything like that. He is pretty plain, in fact. He smiles at me and his slightly crooked teeth glow white in the moonlight.

"Sorry about the trap." He holds out a hand to me. "Your sister insisted. She was worried your Pop would try to slit my throat while I slept if he thought I was trying to steal anything."

I shake his hand cautiously. It is calloused from climbing and fishing.

"Pop *would* slit your throat while you were sleeping if he knew what you were trying to steal," I tell him.

The man looks at the dagger in my hand and nods. "I'm Nigel," he says. His expression remains friendly. He gestures to the rope ladder. "Want to come up? We can pull out some of those thorns."

I don't like the implication that I need his help for anything. He is a thieving, good-for-nothing hot-air ballooner as far as I'm concerned. I do want to see what he's got in his basket though, so I follow him up, climbing one-handed, pulling thorns with my teeth and spitting them into the night.

Nigel's balloon basket looks pretty ordinary. There are some blankets, disrupted from sleep, a pile of books that have seen better days, a string of dried fish hanging from a rack, smaller baskets, woven out of vines and containing fruit and other foraged foods like garlic bulbs and wild onions. There is a row of old moonshine jugs filled with water and reflecting the sky. From the top of his tree the stars look extra bright. Nigel lights his lantern and motions for me to have a seat.

"So," he says.

"So," I say.

"About your sister," he says.

"You can't have her," I tell him.

This leaves us in silence for a few minutes. I eye him up good and continue to spit thorns, so he knows I mean business. Somewhere in the forest the trees shake with tussling polar bears rummaging for dinner. A colony of bats is dislodged and they skitter off over our heads. Nigel doesn't flinch. I suppose he's become used to this sort of thing.

"Charlie, you can't keep her here forever."

He sounds suspiciously like Jezebel herself. "Is that what you've been telling her?" I ask him, trying to keep the anger out of my voice. "No one is keeping her here. This is *our* island. It's where we belong!"

"People belong where they want to be," Nigel says softly. Like he's afraid my world will come crashing down around me with his words.

I could kill him. Well, maim him at least. He has the nerve that only an infiltrator that does not belong can have. "Go land on your own island and say that," I say, grabbing his jugs of water and throwing them off the side of the basket, so that they shatter on the ground below. "These are our jugs and you are drinking them." I toss the fruit overboard as well. "This is our food you have taken."

He still doesn't look particularly guilty. "I'm an explorer," he says. "The world is mine."

I see a pile of cloth folded up to one side with sewing needles and thread. I can guess at the colors. He is repairing his turrets. Soon he will be airborne again. The thought of Jezebel sailing away with him strikes real panic in me.

"All right," I say. "You can have some treasure. Gold, silver, diamonds. I will bring you whatever you want. Just leave my sister behind."

He shakes his head at me. "You can't blame a girl for wanting to see the world," he says. "And you can't blame a guy for falling in love with your sister."

I should shank him. I know I should. Pop would be disgusted by what happens next. Tears, hot and fat, well up in my eyes. I think of things that make me angry. Things to make the tears go away. Things that will make me ready to slit Nigel's throat. Nothing comes. All I can think about is summers without Jezebel. Winters without her. Nighttime ramblings and booby trapping without her. My face is wet.

I hop out of the balloon basket and scale the ladder before Nigel has time to react. I race through the forest, oblivious to traps and tripwires, wandering polar bears, or particularly persistent tourist encampments.

I'm going to tell Pop. I'll let him do what I can't.

But when I reach the house, Pop is passed out across the kitchen table over a string of pearls, his night vision goggles slipped to one side. He is snoring enough to bring the walls down. I knock on

Jezebel's door but she doesn't answer. I do the most shameful thing I have ever done, and cry myself to sleep with my favorite crown on.

In the morning, it is Pop who shakes me awake. "Come see, Charlie. That pickle-brained dope has finally left the island."

I shake doubloons off me and take off my crown.

"Wake up your sister so she can see," he says. He grins, swigs leftovers from a mug of last night's rum, and heads out into the clear morning.

I don't knock on Jezebel's door. I don't bother. Instead I go after Pop and we walk down to the beach where tourists are lined up along the water's edge for a good look.

The castle has been patched up and the turrets are erected into the chilly morning air. It is a cold wind that meets me. The first wind of winter. It makes the crowd shiver and gives speed to the monstrous balloon.

Pop's eyes aren't too good but I know he can see the shock of orange hair that is Jezebel. She is waving goodbye to us from above the ocean.

For a moment Pop is rendered speechless, and then he breaks into such a terrible fit of obscenities and vulgar threats that the crowd on the shore dissipates. The last of the summer treasure hunters pack up their belongings and make for the sea.

Pop is inconsolable. He rants. He raves. He fights a polar bear. He breaks everything in the house. He tears trees straight out of their sockets. He goes on a rum bender for at least a week. I do my best to avoid him for most of this time.

Then one day he simply disappears. He takes the good boat that we hide in a cave at the southern tip of the island. I don't know where he's gone. To sell treasure, or maybe to rescue Jezebel. I find myself staring at the wintry sky a lot, and looking for colored banners and streamers on the horizon with a spyglass. I don't find any. I try to keep to my usual routine. Checking traps, exploring caves, counting treasure.

When Pop reappears he is not alone. He pulls the boat right up onto the sand at Dead Man's Cove and jumps ashore proudly, his chest thrown out like he's staking a claim.

"Charlie!" he calls and I rush down to greet him. He spits out his pirate falsies and puts them in his pocket. "Get us some rum. We are having a celebration!"

A girl climbs out of the boat from behind him. She is smaller than Jezebel and younger too. Her eyes are huge. In her hands are gems, tons of them, glittering different colors in the pale sunlight.

"Meet your new sister, Calliope. Calliope, this here's Charlie. He's going to teach you all about wolf traps, and squirrel snares, and hangman's nooses."

Calliope smiles at me. "Hello."

"Nice to meet you," I say back.

"Is it true this island is full of treasure?"

I nod and Pop looks pleased. He belches and smiles a big, gappy grin.

ViTAL: A LOVE STORY
ALLY MaLineNKO

IF THERE IS NO REFERENCE POINT it's nearly impossible to tell how fast you're traveling. That's one of the first things you notice about deep space. The second is that when galaxies or, in this case, anything else arrives, they arrive quickly.

"Commander?"

"Yes MAC?" I ask, still standing on the platform in front of all that black. It seems to go on forever, and according to our research it does. The universe is expanding faster than we can track it. One day though, it will stop. And then it will contract, fold in on itself, warping time and space, pulling itself back together, undoing the Big Bang with the Big Crunch. And then it will all be over.

"A reading of your vitals says you didn't take your pill this morning?"

"I have it here," I say, staring down at the little orange pill in my palm. Longevity pills.

"L pills need to be taken within a four-hour timeframe."

"I know that MAC." I know it's not possible, but his voice sounds concerned. As if he was capable of emotion, of empathy. As if "he" were an actual he. I toss the pill in my mouth and swallow. "See?" I say. "All gone."

I know he can track the pill though my system without even touching me. Everything about this ship is state of the art. It's an honor to be selected. I knew that. And it still is, even now, even so far from home, so far from my own galaxy. I still believe in the mission. What little boy didn't dream of going to space? To be picked for a Longevity Mission was the highest possible honor. I still wake each morning with the same delicious feeling that today could be the day that I find what I was sent out here to find. Except that hasn't been the case. Not for one hundred years.

"Commander?"

"Yes, MAC?"

"Are you exercising or would you like nutrition?"

"Exercising."

MAC says "nutrition" instead of "food" because we don't have food. But we do have nutrition. Prior to my mission, I hadn't eaten meat in ten years. And yet, out here, all I want is a hamburger. Nutrition, like longevity, comes in pill form. So do mood stabilizers, but I stopped taking those a long time ago. The stabilizers made it easier not to miss things, like food (and conversation with actual people), but I found that wanting things like that reminded me that I was here, alive, in this moment. Being alone for so long, you can forget those things.

"Commander?"

"Yes, MAC?" I ask, hopping onto the treadmill, pulling off my shirt and applying the sensors across my chest. MAC will do a full body analysis, make sure everything is functioning as it should be.

"There is something coming in over the satellite com."

"It's probably gravity static from an asteroid."

"I don't believe it is, Commander."

"Turn it up," I say, picking up the speed on the treadmill. MAC dials up the volume and it takes a second before it fills my ship. It's music. Classical music.

"This is what you're picking up?" I ask.

"Yes."

We'd sent out tons of eggs over the years — capsules full of information for any possible life form. They were filled with a history of our way of life, our planet. Messages in bottles tossed into the deepest reaches of space. We had never retrieved one — never had a response from them. That's why the manned missions were started. That's why I was here.

"It's probably just an egg," I say.

"Negative, Commander. Listen." MAC turns down the reverb on the violins. "Behind the music is this."

I stop jogging. Strain my ears but I don't hear anything. "MAC you have to dial it up. What are you reading?"

"The sinusoidal wave is at 180 hertz."

"That's impossible." I pull the sensors off me, and put my shirt back on.

"I'm afraid you are incorrect, Commander. The fundamental frequency is in fact 180 hertz."

"Music doesn't play at 180 hertz."

"Correct."

"Dial it all the way up, MAC." I wonder if I'll even be able to hear it with my heart beating in my chest the way it is. But there it is. Soft at first, then louder. It's the sound of a woman humming along to the piece that was playing.

"Are you getting a reading?" I ask.

"Indeed, sir."

"Show me."

When the image flashes up on the screen my breath catches. It's a Z-82 Airbird. The exact same model as my ship. It was another Longevity Commander. I can't help but run the numbers in my head, the likelihood, or more so the sheer impossibility that I would run into another Longevity Commander out in all this space.

"This isn't possible," I say.

"Negative, Commander. The likelihood of finding another Z-82 is one in —"

"A trillion," I answer.

"Correct, Commander."

How many times had I sent out that call? In the beginning I would sit in the chair and randomly press that button, the one that sends out a beacon searching for another Commander.

It never found anything. And now, I've just run right into another AirBird.

"Can you patch into its com?" I ask MAC. It's a stupid question. Of course he can.

"We're in," MAC says. There is a feedback-like squeal that fills the ship.

"Connect with the operating system and send a link request."

"Link confirmed and approved."

I lean over the microphone and say, "This is Commander Shield. Do you copy?"

There is another high squeal of feedback before I hear a voice. A woman's voice. "Evening, Commander. This is Commander Evans."

My heart is racing in my ears. There are so many things I want to ask her I'm not even sure where to start.

"I can only see you on the satellite," she says. "How long you expect until we have visual confirmation?"

"Send MAC your coordinates."

They flash on the screen, mapping out her path. Evans just left the galactic center of Abell 4415. Based on her current course in two months we'll pass each other.

"So it looks like we're destined to meet after all?" Evans says. Her laugh bounces off the walls of my ship and suddenly I feel faint. I run the numbers again. I try not to think about how long it's been since I've heard another human voice.

We talk. We trade stories about life back home. That fills the first week. I stand up on the platform edge waiting to see her ship appear in the darkness. But for now it's just dotted with the stars of the galaxies before me.

We talk. Constantly. All day and well into the night. Or what we call night which is really just logged rest hours. In the second week, after we've already said goodbye, her voice comes back on.

"Commander? Are you sleeping?"

I open my eyes, lift my head towards the platform. Still just blackness. "No, what is it? Are you all right?"

"Have you ever thought about why you did this?"

"The mission?"

"Yes."

"It's an honor," I say.

"Company line. Tell me the truth."

I sigh and get out of my pod. As soon as I move, MAC fires up.

"You are awake, Commander."

"It's fine MAC." I tell him. "I'm just talking."

He runs a diagnosis of my vitals, an image of my body appears on the screen.

"Commander Shield?" Evans asks again.

"I'm here."

"You didn't answer my question."

"I did it because it's the chance of a lifetime. I did it because I'll see things that no one else will ever see. I've been traveling the universe for over a hundred years now. It's an honor."

"Alone."

"Excuse me?"

"You've been traveling the universe alone."

Not any more, I almost say but don't.

"The chance of our paths crossing is incredible, you know?" Her voice is soft.

"I know," I say, but so quietly I doubt her com even picked it up.

"It's just incredible, you showing up now."

"Why's that?" I ask, still gazing out in the dark.

"I almost... I've been thinking about... you know, not."

"Not." I repeat. I close my eyes. Hadn't I also been thinking about not?

"Yeah," she says.

"How long have you been out here, if I can ask."

"350 years."

"My god, that's... that's... incredible."

Evans laughs and the sound of it makes my stomach flutter.

I think about the longevity pills. It's always been our choice. We take them. Or we don't. The mission lasts as long as we want it to. When we're done, when we're ready to not, we just stop taking them. It doesn't take long and it's utterly painless. Our ships return to port on their own. They will be empty by then. Our bodies will be disposed of before docking.

"I'm glad you didn't," I say. Evans doesn't answer and I fumble. "I mean, for all that you've seen and sent back to home. The distance you've mapped. It's ..." I struggle for a word. "Vital."

"Vital. Yes."

I think of those men, millennia ago, who set sail and mapped our home world. We are cut from the same stone. There is something that keeps driving us forward, constantly. We leave our own lives behind just to know what's out there.

"Commander?" she says.

"Yes."

"I apologize for waking you. I'm going to get some rest now."

"Okay."

"We'll talk tomorrow."

"Of course."

We talk every day. She sends me data from her journeys to galaxies I haven't seen yet. I send her mine. Neither of us has ever found any sign of an alien life. Never a blip on the screen, never another ship. Nothing but space.

We make jokes.

She makes me laugh.

Each day I watch the blackness for signs of her ship. When we map our paths again, we see that we are seventy-two hours from passing.

"How close will we be?" I ask but what I want to ask is *Will I be able to see you?*

"MAC calculates that we'll pass within fifteen feet of each other. Will you be on the platform, Commander?"

"Enough with the Commander. Please call me —"

"No," Evans yells. "Don't tell me your name. I don't want to know until I see you."

"But when we are within that range, our frequencies will overload. We won't be able to talk. The coms will go static."

"I know."

We come up with a plan.

I can see her ship from the platform now. A silver orb wobbling in all that dark. I don't feel like a Commander watching her ship get closer. I feel like a teenage boy, going on his first date.

MAC warns me that communication is going to cut off soon.

"Commander?" I say.

"Yes?"

"I guess this is goodbye for a while."

She laughs. "Oddly enough it's also hello."

I smile. The static builds.

"I'll see you soon," she says.

"Yes." There are so many things I want to tell her. I almost try but then the static screams through the ship and I tell MAC to dial it down for god's sake. I can see the nose of her craft clearly now. Soon our platforms will face each other and then I will see her. I stand at the furthest end so that as we pass, I can walk the distance of the wide window. So that I can see her for as long as possible.

"Pull the panels back, MAC," I say and he does. The solar panels that protect me contract and now the window doubles in size. The nose of her ship fills my view and I gasp at the sheer size of it.

Her platform window comes in to view and there she is. Dressed in the same Commander blues as me. Her hair is cut in a shoulder-length bob. She smiles at me. I laugh with the sheer joy of seeing her, alive, in front of me. She mouths the word "hi" and gives me a little wave. I do the same.

Ready? she mouths.

I nod.

We each hold up the signs we created.

On mine I've written Eirik.

On hers, Monica.

Hi Monica, I mouth.

She laughs, her head thrown back and my stomach summersaults. We have to start walking now as our ships pass. She presses her hand up against the glass of her platform window and I do the same. It feels, for a brief moment, like I'm actually touching her and the sensation makes me dizzy. I close my eyes for a second and then open them, terrified of missing something. I can feel myself shaking. She's so beautiful and alive and right here. She must be thinking something similar because she wipes at a tear. Monica is younger than me. She must have made Commander early. So smart. So brave. Monica.

My Monica.

I suddenly love her so much. I remember everything we've talked about this last month. I remember why I did this to begin with. I think of all those people back home, and how they are sleepwalking through their life. How they don't appreciate every single second they're given. Every single beautiful person they are privileged to know. Monica reminds me of that just by being here, alive in all that stretching darkness. How lucky we are, just to even have this moment together.

I want to tell her all of this. But instead I tell her I love her.

Her smile widens. I love you, too, she mouths.

I've reached the end of my platform now. I press myself against the window wishing I could slow our ships down.

"Goodbye," she mouths.

"Hello," I say and then again, she laughs.

Her ship passes completely and darkness fills my window. I sit down and think about Monica. About how lucky I am. I feel dizzy with joy.

"Commander?"

"Yes, MAC?"

"Communication link has been restored."

"Hi, Eirik." Monica's voice fills my cabin.

"Hi, Monica."

"I think that might have been the best moment of my life."

"Me too."

What now? I wonder but don't want to say. We'll probably have another month or so before we're too far apart and our link is broken. Instead I tell her a story about the letters that Captain James Cook used to drop into the sea as he sailed to the bottom of the world. He addressed each one to his wife, Elizabeth. After he died exploring the Hawaiian Islands, they say she waited out on the shores of England for the bottles to return to her.

"That's a sad story," Monica tells me and I can hear that it's upset her.

"It would be," I tell her, "if she never found the bottles."

Monica laughs a bit, clears her throat. "Now you're just making things up."

"No, I tell her. It's the truth. When Elizabeth died, amongst her possessions were three letters from Captain Cook. All dated while he was at sea. It's been authenticated. Somehow he found a way to still talk to her. A way to love her. A way for them to still be connected even over all that distance."

"I like that," Monica says.

"Good. You keep taking those longevity pills, okay?"

"You too," and then after a beat she says, "It's a big galaxy though. I mean the chance of us seeing …"

"Not that big. Not impossibly big. Not so big that two people won't see each other again. No bigger than the ocean was for James and Elizabeth, right?"

ABOUT THE CONTRIBUTORS

NICOLA BELTE lives in Birmingham, U.K, and has never dressed up as a woodland creature. When NOT doing that, she writes fiction, and you can find her at her blog: nicolabelte.blogspot.com.

JACKSON BURGESS is a writer, painter, and student at the University of Southern California. His work has been or will be published in places, including recently *Corvus Magazine*, *Petrichor Machine*, and *Subliminal Interiors*. You can find him wandering around South Central LA, often with paint-stained hands. To see his full publishing history or to make sure he's still alive, visit his personal blog: jacksonburgess.wordpress.com.

DANGER SLATER is the world's most flammable writer! He writes with a lot of exclamation points! He is your favorite writer! You love him! He is the author of *Love Me* and half of *Stranger Danger*. His newest book is *I Will Rot Without You*, available from Fungasm Press right the hell now. Here is his website: dangerslater.blogspot.com.

BEN NARDOLILLI currently lives in New York City. His work has appeared in *Perigee Magazine*, *Red Fez*, *Danse Macabre*, *The 22 Magazine*, *Quail Bell Magazine*, *Elimae*, *fwriction*, *THEMA*, *Pear Noir*, *The Minetta Review*, and *Yes Poetry*. He blogs at mirrorsponge.blogspot.com and is looking to publish a novel.

ALLY MALINENKO is the author of the poetry collections, *The Wanting Bone* (Six Gallery Press) and *How To Be An American* (Six Gallery Press) as well as the novel, *This is Sarah* (BookFish Books). Forthcoming work includes *Better Luck Next Year* (Low Ghost Press). She tweets at @allymalinenko mostly about Doctor Who.

J.D. HAGER lives in Northern California with his wife, his dogs, and a small collection of farm animals. He spends his days working undercover as a middle school science teacher and school garden coordinator. His fiction has appeared in the *Porter Gulch Review*, *Bartleby Snopes*, *Cease Cows*, *East of the Web*, and is forthcoming in many other places.

YVONNE YU is a Brown University undergraduate and the co-creator of the hashtag BadBitchLipClub. She currently works as a sexual health educator and advocate. A fan of the obscure and the macabre, she keeps her wisdom teeth in a glass display case and would like others to believe that she once killed a man. Previously published in *The Molotov Cocktail*, she is learning to stop whining and just keep writing.

YT SUMNER likes words and people that write them. People that listen to them. People that read them. Eavesdroppers. Stutterers. Silvertongues. She was born in the U.K., raised all over Australia and settled happily in Melbourne. Her short stories have appeared in various literary journals, anthologies and magazines and she's currently coaxing a motley group of them into a collection. Visit her at lambeatswolf.wordpress.com and then send her a postcard.

CHRISTOPHER LETTERA hears noises in the night woods. Voices on CB radios. Bats, maybe. A former lifeguard and video store clerk, he currently teaches poetry and Mythology in English Literature at Youngstown State University. He is the recipient of the Robert R. Hare Award for fiction and placed as runner-up in the Ohio River Valley chapter of the recent NSAL short story writing competition. His short fiction has appeared most recently in *Crack the Spine* and is forthcoming in *Literary Orphan's Best of* print anthology.

CHRISTOPHER DeWAN has written numerous short stories, recently featured in *Apocrypha and Abstractions, Bartleby Snopes, Bewildering Stories, Fractured West, In Between Altered States, MicroHorror, Necessary Fiction*, and *Niteblade*. In 2012, was a contributor at the Bread Loaf Writers' Conference, and his short story "The Garden" was nominated for a 2013 Pushcart Prize.

LIZ KICAK lives in Tampa, Florida. She received her MFA from the University of South Florida and is now the Assistant Director of the school's Humanities Institute. Her poetry has appeared in *New York Quarterly*, *Barely South Review*, *The Tulane Review*, *Southern Women's Review*, *Palooka Literary Review*, and others.

ANNA LEA JANCEWICZ lives in Norfolk, Virginia, where she homeschools her children and haunts the public libraries. If she could fistfight any historical figure, it'd probably be Martin Luther or Herman Melville. Also, she has no familial feelings toward her dog. Her writing has recently appeared at *Bartleby Snopes*, *The Citron Review*, *Rawboned*, *Squalorly*, and elsewhere. Yes, you CAN say Jancewicz: Yahnt-SEV-ich. More at annajancewicz.wordpress.com

SLOAN THOMAS lives on an Indian reservation in Northern California. She enjoys listening to not-so-tall tales of old Indians and small children. She has work published in *Word Riot* and *SmokeLong Quarterly* under the name R.S. Thomas.

MICHAEL SIONS is a Richmond, Virginia, native, studying architecture at the University of Virginia. He would've studied literature, but literature majors don't make as much money as architects. He enjoys listening to rap and has been known to freestyle a verse or two when the time is right. His sense of humor often falls spectacularly flat in conversation due to the fact that he seems to be the only person on this entire planet with an unbreakable conviction that, regardless of the circumstances, elephants are always funny. Always.

MATTHEW MYERS studied film at New York University in the 90s but somehow ended up working on an ambulance in the Midwest. He now works in an office, where the leftover adrenaline from his past profession has been redirected and is now secreted as fiction of both short- and long-range capability. Apart from one accidental short-form publication, this is his first published work.

GRAHAM TUGWELL is a writer and performer. The recipient of the College Green Literary Prize 2010, he enjoys writing work of abiding strangeness, aimed at provoking that apocalyptic oscillation where the brain cannot decide what is appropriate — laughter or grief. He has lived his whole life in the village where all his stories take place. He loves it with a very special type of hate.

KIMBERLY LOJEWSKI received her MFA in fiction from UMass Amherst. Her first book, *Worm Fiddling Nocturne in the Key of a Broken Heart*, is being released by Burrow Press in 2016. She has been published in *PANK*, *Gargoyle*, *Drunken Boat*, and elsewhere, and her stories have been nominated for several Pushcarts as well as winning Best of the Net by Sundress Publications.

ABOUT THE PUBLISHER

THE JERSEY DEVIL IS A CREATURE OF LEGEND, lurking in the shadows of the Pine Barrens of southern New Jersey, revealing itself only to wreak havoc on some small town, snack on some poor, unsuspecting chicken or goat, and, occasionally, if it's feeling a little randy, to hit on mermaids down the Jersey shore.

Jersey Devil Press, on the other hand, is a small independent publisher, born on the toll roads and raised in the diners of that great Garden State, revealing itself only to release a monthly online magazine of short fiction, publish the occasional novel or story collection, and, sometimes, if it's feeling a little frisky, to write gratuitous run-on sentences and publicly decry the downfall of humanity that is *Jersey Shore*.

Check out our free monthly online magazine at:
www.jerseydevilpress.com

www.ingramcontent.com/pod-product-compliance
Lightning Source LLC
Chambersburg PA
CBHW030633130626
46552CB00002B/836